BAYOU BARGAIN

"You are a brave man, Skye Fargo," Nannine said. "We believe here in the bayou that to be close to the brave is to share some of their bravery."

Nannine lifted her arms high and with one quick motion, whisked her shift off to stand absolutely naked before him. Slowly Skye took in the lithe, coffee-with-milk body, her breasts curving upwards with saucy impudence. His eyes scanned below at a thimble-sized waist and hips that flared in sudden womanliness. But it was her legs, long, slender stalks, that formed the finishing touch in a symphony of sepia sensuousness.

If this bayou beauty wanted some of his courage, Skye thought as Nannine reached out to unbuckle his belt, he reckoned they'd be able to work out a trade. . . .

THE
SWAMP SLAYERS

by
Jon Sharpe

A SIGNET BOOK

NEW AMERICAN LIBRARY

PUBLISHER'S NOTE

This novel is a work of fiction. Names, characters, places, and incidents either are the product of the author's imagination or are used fictitiously, and any resemblance to actual persons, living or dead, events, or locales is entirely coincidental.

The first chapter of this book previously appeared in *The White Hell Trail*, the forty-eighth volume in this series.

SIGNET TRADEMARK REG. U.S. PAT. OFF. AND FOREIGN COUNTRIES
REGISTERED TRADEMARK—MARCA REGISTRADA
HECHO EN CHICAGO, U.S.A.

SIGNET, SIGNET CLASSIC, MENTOR, PLUME, MERIDIAN
AND NAL BOOKS are published by New American Library,
1633 Broadway, New York, New York 10019

First Printing, January, 1986

1 2 3 4 5 6 7 8 9

PRINTED IN THE UNITED STATES OF AMERICA

The Trailsman

Beginnings . . . they bend the tree and they mark the man. Skye Fargo was born when he was eighteen. Terror was his midwife, vengeance his first cry. Killing spawned Skye Fargo, ruthless, cold-blooded murder. Out of the acrid smoke of gunpowder still hanging in the air, he rose, cried out a promise never forgotten.

The Trailsman, they began to call him, all across the West: searcher, scout, hunter, the man who could see where others only looked, his skills for hire but not his soul, the man who lived each day to the fullest, yet trailed each tomorrow. Skye Fargo, the Trailsman, the seeker who could take the wildness of a land and the wanting of a woman and make them his own.

The Louisiana back country,
near the dark and secret places
known as the bayous . . .

"Now, you're much too pretty a little thing to be hold-ing such a big, ugly gun," Skye Fargo said soothingly. But it was no quick-talk compliment. The lamp the girl had set down on the cellar floor showed that she was both small and pretty, dark-blond hair, an even-featured face, a nice, small nose, and beautifully formed lips. But it was her eyes that held him, blue fires that seemed to burn with a strange light.

"Now, you just put that rifle down and we can talk nice and proper," Fargo said.

The big, lever-action Volcanic didn't move so much as a fraction of an inch, he saw.

"Throw your gun down," the girl said.

Fargo hesitated and saw the rifle barrel lift to point directly at his gut. She was too close to miss, and the big Volcanic could blow a buffalo apart at this range. Slowly, he lifted the Colt from its holster and let it slide to the floor. A tremendous bolt of lightning illu-minated the cellar with a flash of blue-white light, and the thunderclap shook the house. He saw that the girl had moved a few paces from the stairs that led up to the first floor.

"I told you, I can explain," Fargo said. "I came in to get out of the storm. Christ, you can hear it's something fearful out there. I was lost." The girl said nothing and he went on quickly. "The house seemed deserted. I called out, tried the front door. Nobody answered. I went around and found the storm-cellar entrance."

The burning blue eyes seemed to pierce right through him. She wore an almost-floor-length loose shift that hid most of her body under its shapelessness, yet two round, high mounds managed to push into the garment. "Maybe that's the way it was. Maybe not," she said flatly.

"That's just the way it was. I'm telling you the truth," Fargo said.

"Doesn't make any difference," she said almost wearily.

"What do you mean? Of course it makes a difference," Fargo protested.

He saw her shoulders lift in a half-shrug. "You're a dead man either way," she said. She lifted her voice, called out without taking her eyes from him. Or the big rifle, either, he noted. "Igor," she called.

Fargo's eyes went to the top of the stairs as he saw the shadow appear first, then the figure step into view. His frown dug deeper into his brow. The man started down the steps, filling every inch of the stairway, a mountainous figure nearly seven feet tall, Fargo guessed. The giant's shaven head barely cleared the timbers of the roof of the cellar. Small eyes in the heavy face peered at him, a slightly Mongol cast to their shape. The giant wore knee-length, baggy trousers, his chest and arms bare except for a small, embroidered vest that hardly covered the upper part of his torso. Fargo took in a tremendous chest, arms the size of small trees, a belly carrying perhaps ten pounds too much fat. The hulk was awesome, frightening in size and manner as he reached the floor of the cellar of the house and started to lumber forward.

"He's yours, Igor. Enjoy yourself," the girl said.

No small man himself, Fargo felt dwarfed by the hulk and cast a quick glance at the girl. She had stepped back closer to the stairs, but the burning blue eyes looked on excitedly.

"What the hell is this?" Fargo flung at her. "You get your kicks by watching this mountain fall on people?" He peered at her and saw no change in the pretty face as the burning blue eyes continued to watch. He flicked a glance at the Colt on the floor. The huge figure saw the glance, kicked the gun with one foot, and sent it skittering into a corner of the cellar. Fargo moved backward slowly as his eyes scanned the cellar and took in old brass-fitted trunks, wooden crates, an odd bedstand, broken barrels—all the odd and castaway things that find their way into cellars.

He brought his eyes back to the huge figure that lumbered toward him in the dim light of the lamp. Fargo's lips were a thin, tight line as he backed away. None of it made any damn sense. The girl had just cast aside his explanation. But he hadn't time to wonder about that now. He had to think about staying alive, and he went into a weaving crouch as the huge figure came at him. The giant lifted his huge arms, bulged powerful shoulder muscles, and tried a long, looping left. Fargo dodged it easily, avoided the right that followed, and threw a sharp right cross that landed on the giant's jaw. It was a blow that would have sent most men down, but the huge figure didn't even pause in his lumbering gait.

Fargo ducked another looping blow, drove a whistling uppercut under the man's jaw. This time Igor made a grunting sound as his head snapped back, but

11

he plowed forward again instantly. Fargo moved under another ponderous blow to throw a counter right and saw, in surprise, the tremendous downward blow come at him with a sudden explosion of speed. He tried to turn away, but the blow caught him on the shoulder and felt as though a tree had fallen on him. He fell sideways and stumbled, and another powerful blow caught him in the side. He hit the cellar floor, spun, and regained his feet just in time to avoid a bone-crushing kick. Off balance from the missed kick, the giant figure almost fell forward, and Fargo brought a whistling blow around in a flat arc and drove his fist deep into the giant's kidney.

The blow would have collapsed anyone else, and Igor did let out a roar of pain as he spun around. But he came forward again, his little eyes glittering with rage. Fargo feinted, started a hard right, and drew back as he saw the giant's sledgehammer fist poised. The huge man was deceptive, he had learned. His lumbering could explode into astonishing bursts of speed, and Fargo backed from a long left, ducked under another, tried a counterblow, and swung away without delivering it as Igor's huge fist exploded. The swish of air grazed the top of his head as he ducked, pulled away, and watched the brute come at him again.

Igor leapt with a sudden rush and Fargo spun to one side to avoid a treelike arm and drove a powerful left into the brute's solar plexus. Igor staggered, drew breath in hard, but didn't go down. Fargo brought a hard right up onto the man's jaw, and Igor's head went back. He was wearing the giant down, he told himself, and he stepped in again, his confidence misleading him. The downward blow arced over him with another explosion of speed, and he whirled to avoid it and felt the blow slam into him between the

12

shoulder blades. He hit the floor facedown, his back burning with pain. He rolled, but the kick caught him on the arm and sent him crashing into a trunk. He tried to roll again, but there was no space and the huge hands closed around him, pulled him up, and lifted him into the air.

The giant flung him as though he were a doll, and he smashed into the wall with a force that jarred every bone in his body. He dropped to the floor against the wall. He didn't try to meet the hulk's next blow but catapulted himself forward. Igor, expecting him to try to cover up, had barreled forward, and Fargo heard his bellow of rage and pain as he smashed into the wall. Fargo fought away the pain of his own body as he rolled and pulled himself to his feet.

Another flash of lightning flooded the cellar for an instant, and Fargo saw the girl beside the stairs, her burning blue eyes fixed on the battle, her lips parted in excitement. Goddamn little bitch, Fargo swore silently as the surge of fury spiraled through him. The hulk raced toward him again and this time Fargo waited in a crouch, every muscle tensed. He measured distances and let the huge hands almost reach his throat. He dropped onto all fours, and Igor's tremendous bulk fell over him to crash to the floor. Fargo rose, leapt up into the air, and came down with both feet on the giant's back.

Igor let out a roar of pain, and Fargo jumped to the side as the huge figure rolled over and started to pull himself to his feet. Fargo stared in astonishment as the giant rose up, towered into the air with his back plainly not broken. Igor dived forward, and Fargo threw a blazing right that connected with the man's jaw. The giant staggered, and Fargo delivered a whistling left cross, saw the brute leap into the air and his blow harmlessly bounce off the giant's chest. He tried to duck aside but Igor's mountainous form crashed down on him and he felt himself go down. Igor seized him from behind, lifted him again, and flung him in a sideways arc. Fargo landed half over a big, solid trunk and gasped out in pain.

He let himself go over the top and fall onto the other side of the trunk, a narrow space near the wall. He glimpsed the broken handle of a shovel on the floor, seized it, and swung from behind the trunk as the giant's treelike arms reached across for him. His blow caught the man along the side of his head, and Igor drew back in pain. He swung one tremendous arm in a backhand motion and smashed it against the broken shovel handle. The weapon flew out of Fargo's hand. Fargo watched it skitter along the floor and he half-dived, half-leapt around the end of the trunk and fell on it, rolled, came up with the length of heavy wood again.

Igor charged—a rush worthy of a wounded buffalo—head down, massive bulk hurtling. Fargo swung his weapon in an upward arc. Igor glimpsed it and managed to twist his head, but the blow ripped up alongside his temple and a gush of blood erupted, to run down the side of his head. Fargo ducked away from the giant, brought the length of wood crashing down on the shaven head. The broken handle splintered as it landed, and Igor went down. He dropped to both knees and hung there with his bleeding head moving from side to side, not unlike a grizzly gathering itself.

Fargo clasped both hands together, raised them over his head, and brought them down onto the back of Igor's neck with all his remaining strength. The hulk fell face forward onto the floor, lay there, a twitching mountain. He wasn't dead, only unconscious, his temple making a red puddle on the cellar floor. Fargo dropped to one knee to draw in deep, rasping breaths. He looked up to see the girl move toward him from the stairs, the rifle firmly pointed at him.

"Enjoy it, damn your hide?" Fargo gasped out between breaths.

"Yes," she said softly, excitement in the burning blue eyes, her lips slightly parted. "Very impressive. I've never seen anyone stand up to Igor, much less beat him."

"There's a first time for everything," Fargo spit out as he stayed on one knee and let his breath return.

"Too bad," the girl said, her pretty face expressionless.

"What's that mean?" Fargo growled.

"Too bad it was all for nothing," she said.

"All for nothing? Goddamn, I won. What the hell more do you want?" Fargo roared.

He saw her aim the rifle. "All for nothing," she repeated, and he dived, flung himself flat as he did so. "Goddamn bitch," he snarled as he hit the floor and felt the blast of rifle fire brush across his back. He rolled, scrambled for the corner where the Colt lay. He had almost reached it when her second shot rang out, and he felt the sharp, searing pain shoot through his head. He seemed on fire, a split-second burst of excruciating flame that vanished to leave nothing, neither pain nor sense nor feeling. The world ceased to exist.

Mists rose from the still waters to allow only a glimpse of trailing, tangled vines. Tall, knobby-kneed trees reached upward out of the watery depths to disappear into the mists, and long, sinuous tendrils hung down as if suspended in midair. Noth-

15

ing seemed to move and yet there was life here, the air filled with a scent faintly musky yet sweet, hanging moss and mimosa, humus and hyacinth. In this place, it was as though time had stood still and a dark, deep silence seemed to own the world.

But something jarred this hanging quiet, something foreign disturbed its primeval beauty. Near the center of one watery passageway, an object lay against the roots of a bald cypress, more in the water than out. The object stirred, became a figure, shirt caught against the edge of a splintered knot in the tree trunk. It was the only thing that kept the figure's head out of the water as morning began to seep its way through the dense strands of hanging moss. Skye Fargo's eyelids twitched. It was the first sign of existence that he'd had since the rifle blast struck. He moved his eyelids again, forced them to pull open.

The effort sent waves of pain rushing through his head, and he lay still. But the pain refused to go away. He kept his eyes open, tried to focus, but he saw only formless areas of color as the pain throbbed through his head. He felt his body immersed in wetness, and he tried to think back. The rifle blast was all he could remember. There had been nothing after that. He forced himself to stare into space, and slowly the formless pieces of color began to take shape. He made out trees, water, long, hanging tendrils. The world began to reappear, and he glanced down to see his body almost completely submerged in the dull-green water.

He lifted his arm, stopped at once as the pain shot through his body. The faint movement sent water lapping against his face. He forced down the waves of pain to raise his head. He felt his shirt slip from the splintered piece of tree trunk that had held him. He reached up, almost cried out in pain, and caught hold of the knobby knees of the cypress that protruded from the water, and held himself in place. He lowered his head as the pain swept through him.

The rifle blast had injured nerve endings that remained raw and throbbing, and Fargo clung to the perch and let the worst of the pain subside. He let his eyes take in the watery pathways that stretched out on both sides of him, the heavy tendrils hanging beside the moss. He spied a little island that rose up in the water, hardly more than a small mound of sago pondweed. It offered a refuge, a dry haven to rest. He couldn't cling much longer to the smooth tree root, he realized as he felt what little strength he had slipping out of his arms.

He half-turned, saw the dark-gray, knobby log lying mostly submerged in the water but near enough for him to easily reach. Another bumpy gray log lay three-quarters submerged a few yards farther on, and Fargo slowly let himself slide completely into the water. He began to drift slowly. Suddenly, he froze as the nearest log blinked at him. He stared and the log blinked again, and he saw two tiny eyes protruding up in what he'd taken to be knobby, rough bark. The log moved, rose in the water, and at the end nearest him a row of jagged teeth appeared. Fargo swallowed as the log transformed itself into a big, gray alligator, some twelve feet, he guessed, the bumpy gray bark its thick, warty hide.

Fargo's gasped curse lodged in his throat. He had slid from the smooth root of the cypress. He hadn't the strength to try to pull himself back. Besides, it would require too much effort and movement, and that, above all else, would be a fatal mistake. He floated on his back, arms pressed to his side, and tried to lie absolutely still in the water. He saw the other log rise and start to lazily move toward him.

17

Letting only his eyes move, he watched the two alligators swim toward him, hardly rippling the water as they came. The pain still racked his body and his head. One snap of those crushing jaws could end it, but it wasn't a remedy he'd welcome. He watched the two gators half-turn with the barest movement of their tails.

Both swam directly at him, their tiny eyes blinking.

2

Fargo lay motionless as he fought down the impulse to try to get away. The temptation was an invitation to certain death. Even in top condition, he'd never be able to outswim a big gator. He hardly let himself breathe as the two alligators neared him. Reptile, fish, animal, or human would do for a hungry gator's dinner, he knew.

Only his eyes moved as he watched the two huge, warty hides as they swam slowly on either side of him. One brushed his arm with the hard hide of its midsection, and Fargo closed his eyes at the surge of pain that went through him. His entire body seemed a raw, exposed nerve. He remained motionless and kept his eyes open just enough to see the two alligators swim silently on, hardly disturbing the water as they moved away.

Fargo still didn't move, aware that any sudden vibration in the water would bring them back instantly. But he allowed himself a deep breath and felt his body trembling as he drifted toward the little island. He had precious little strength left, he knew, and he fought away the gray curtain that tried to drop down over him again.

The little island of pondweed was nearby, yet it

seemed to take forever to reach. The pain that throbbed throughout his body made him nauseous with its intensity. When he finally came upon the edge of the little island, he lay still for a long moment, his body rubbing gently along the soft rise of the tiny weed-covered knoll. Finally, gathering up all his remaining strength, he curled his fingers around the tough, fibrous resiliency of the pond-weed. He pulled, almost crying out with pain, paused, then forced himself to pull again.

The crawl onto the little mound of soft earth, marsh grass, and staghorn club moss was as strenuous as climbing the Rockies. But he painfully managed his way atop the island. Pain and exhaustion combined to sweep the world away again. The gray curtain fell over him. Once again he lay in unfeeling, unseeing, unknowing timelessness.

Warmth awakened him this time—warmth and a sweet scent. His eyes came open slowly. The warmth remained. The scent, too. He stared into grayness until the curtain dissolved to become shapes, forms, and colors. He found himself staring up at a ceiling, pieces of narrow wood overlapping one another. He looked sideways to take in walls also made of narrow strips of wood with heavy vines in between. He was in a hut of some kind, he decided. He tried to move and winced as he felt the pain again, though less intense now. He looked down to see that he lay naked on a mattress. His eyes traveled around the hut, noting it was one large room illuminated by a big candle in a glass bowl. He saw another large mattress on the other side of the room, a three-legged table, a low chopping block, and a wooden stand holding clay dishes in the corner.

Thoughts whirled inside him as he let his head fall

back on the mattress. One thing was clear: the shot that had struck his head had really only grazed him. Yet it had been close enough to seem fatal, and he drew a deep breath of gratitude. Suddenly he tensed, knew he was not alone. His wild-creature instincts still functioned, he was happy to find. He half-turned and saw the figure standing beside him: a girl, slender, long jet-black hair and eyes to match. She pressed a hand to his forehead and her voice sounded very far away. "Sleep," he heard her say. "Sleep. You hurt bad. Sleep more." It seemed a good idea, and the questions that rose to his lips fell away. He felt his eyes close, saw her figure fade away, and a gray curtain pulled itself over him again as his body sank into the sleep of the exhausted.

A stream of filtered sunlight shining through the open doorway woke him in the morning. He blinked, and the hut came into focus. He lay still a moment and pulled on his memory. Little vignettes floated back to him; the alligators first, then the tiny island where he had found refuge. Dimly he remembered hanging moss, long tendrils, and still waters. The girl came into his mind, her jet-black hair, her hand pressed onto his forehead. Somehow he had gotten from the tiny island to here. He pushed himself up on one elbow just as the girl appeared in the open doorway of the hut. Her black hair streamed midway down her back, and she was wearing a tattered, one-piece shift of dark brown that barely reached to midthigh, revealing slender, shapely legs the color of coffee that was half-milk.

His eyes went to her face, the same light sepia as her legs. A straight nose, sharply molded lips, and strong cheekbones completed a strikingly beautiful face filled with dark fire in its high planes. The muslin shift clung to a very small waist and up to

21

high breasts that pushed against the shift with insouciant curves.

She came toward him and he realized that only a small towel lay across the nakedness at his crotch. She halted, a strange combination of hauteur and wildness, of woman and little girl. She showed gleaming, even teeth in a slow smile that·was both dazzling and full of female wisdom.

"You are one very lucky feller," she said, and he immediately caught the accented inflection of her speech, a hint of French in its musical lilt. "You hurt bad when I find you," she said.

"Where'd you find me?" he asked.

"On the little island. You lucky there, too." She laughed, a chiding quality in the sound. "Shot almost kill you."

"Why?" Fargo queried.

"Plenty gators take sun there," she said.

His eyes met the jet-black orbs that seemed to dance with tiny black fires. "How long have I been here?" he asked.

"Two days," the girl said as her eyes moved up and down his body with approval and appreciation. "You recover very quick," she added solemnly.

"You brought me here?" Fargo asked.

"With my two little brothers," she said. "You die on the little island if the gators don't eat you alive."

"Then I owe you my life," he said. "Who are you?"

"Nannine," she said.

"I'm Fargo. Skye Fargo," he said. "It seems you're a wonderful healer, Nannine."

"I use old creole recipe." The girl smiled. "Vervain, melilot, yerba mansa, and witch hazel. Salve and poultices both." She knelt down beside him and put both hands onto his shoulders. Slowly she moved them down across his chest, over the flat, hard-muscled belly, down farther, and halted at the edge of the towel. Then she drew her hands away, and he thought he caught laughter inside her jet orbs.

"Good. You are cool," she said. "How do you come here?" she asked.

He frowned as thoughts flashed into his mind for a brief instant. "I was dumped here," he said. "Just where am I?"

"You are in the bayou country, Fargo," the girl replied.

The young woman rose and went to a corner of the room where a small circle of stones made a fireplace. A small flame burned under a black iron pot. Using a cloth, she grasped the handle of the pot and poured a liquid into a round, earthenware cup.

"Drink," she said as she brought the steaming liquid to him. "Wintergreen hyssop tea. Good for you," she said, and folded herself onto the edge of the mattress.

He sipped the brew and felt its fiery warmth go through him. "You live here, Nannine?" he asked.

"With my little brothers, Jean and Christophe," Nannine said, and stretched her legs out as she leaned back on her elbows. The shift rode up to show long, beautifully curved thighs of smooth sepia. She seemed as unconcerned at revealing her beauty as a cat who shows itself when it stretches. Indeed, there was a feline quality to her, languor cloaking quickness.

"How little?" Fargo asked.

"Jean is ten, Christophe thirteen," she said.

"No folks?" Fargo queried as he sipped the tea.

"Papa and Mama? They live on the other side of the bayous," Nannine said, and he watched the upwardly curved, saucy breasts push hard against the square top of the brown shift.

"Why do you and your brothers live out here?" he asked with honest curiosity.

"They fish their bayou. We do this one. That way there are two cabins bringing the écrevisse, crevettes, and tortue to market," she said.

"The last one is turtle. What are the other two?" Fargo asked.

"You call them crawfish and prawn." Nannine laughed, swung her slender body around in a graceful arc, and bounded to her feet. The shift clung to her with a provocativeness that simply refused to acknowledge its own tattered condition. "Your clothes are there if you wish to dress," she said, and gestured to a corner. "I wash them clean, the sun dry them good." She smiled.

"Thanks," Fargo said. He watched her eyes move over his body, a glint of private amusement in their jet-black depths.

She turned, strode to the doorway of the little hut, and flashed a quick smile at him. "I will be back," she said, and vanished through the doorway.

Fargo slowly pushed himself to his feet and stretched, feeling only a twinge of pain. He walked to the corner where his clothes were neatly folded and saw the gun belt with his Colt in the holster. The sight both surprised and jarred him, but it was silent proof of two things. First, the crazy girl and mountain man Igor must have thought him dead or soon to be so when they threw him into the bayou. Second, they'd put the Colt into the holster so there'd be nothing left behind, which meant he'd stumbled onto something and had to be eliminated quickly and thoroughly. It was clear they'd expected the gators or the waters of the bayou to dispose of him effectively.

But he'd been lucky, his shirt catching on the jagged knot of wood and then being rescued by

Nannine. He dressed, strapped on his gun belt, and stepped from the hut to find himself on a narrow dock made of warped planks. It jutted perhaps six feet into the water. His eyes swept the still, mysteriously beautiful avenues of dull green that wandered through the hanging moss and the long vines. Huge cypresses reached up out of the depths as though they were the ghosts of trees.

He sat down at the edge of the short dock and the scent of the hyacinth floated over him. He relaxed his body in the sweet, lazy atmosphere of the bayou as he forced his mind to reel backward. He had to put everything in order again before going on, so he let his thoughts go back to the letter that had brought him here in the first place.

It had been an urgent plea for help from Ned Simmons, once a close friend of his pa. The desperate note written in shaky handwriting told of a missing daughter and a terrible fear. Fargo saw the words again in his mind as he thought back:

It's more than Cynthia, old friend. Other young women have disappeared and it keeps on. There's got to be some signs, a trail, something, but nobody around here's been able to come up with anything. There's not one real good tracker around. Sure as hell, there's nobody like you. My two bad legs keep me from doing much, so I'm asking you for help.

I know this isn't your kind of country, but you're still the very best, the Trailsman as they call you now. Go talk to Joe Alcott. He's in a town called St. Lucifer. His niece disappeared, too, and he's right there on the scene. I told him to expect you and sent him the cash to pay you. Please help us, we sure need it.

That had been the start of it, Fargo recalled. He'd just finished a long drive east to Missouri when

25

Ned's letter caught up to him, and Louisiana and southern belles seemed a welcome change. He remembered thinking how, if it all worked out right, he might just go down to New Orleans afterward. There was a town for real relaxing. He'd posted a note to Ned telling him he'd come down, finished a last few days' work in Missouri, and headed south. He had cut straight down Missouri, skirted the Boston Mountains in Arkansas, and followed the Ouachita down into Louisiana.

He'd been riding the back country, trying to find his way to St. Lucifer, when the storm struck as night fell. No ordinary storm, it had swept down with a savage fury that turned the world into inky blackness with a towering, wind-driven downpour. The fierce lightning flashes illuminated the torrential rains, and he fought his way forward with growing uneasiness. The Louisiana back country was filled with sudden swamplands, he knew, and he was thoroughly lost in a raging storm in a territory he'd never ridden before.

He'd been seeking a place to hole up when a jagged burst of lightning revealed the big house directly in his path. He'd shouted in gratefulness and sent the Ovaro on. Another lightning flash had let him see tall, white columns at the front of the house, a terraced balcony over the tall, arched windows of the ground floor, and round bay windows on the two wings at either side. He slid from the saddle, pulled the Ovaro under the dubious protection of a big willow, and banged on the front door. He'd pounded and called, but his voice had been whipped away by the rainswept winds. He'd made his way to the side of the house when he spotted the storm-cellar entrance. He'd lifted the door, found it open, and let himself down into the dryness of the cellar.

He'd been shaking rainwater from himself when

the girl appeared with the lamp. She had come down the stairs from the floor above, and Fargo felt anger surge through him as he thought about her. Vicious little sadist, he muttered. She'd wanted to see him beaten to a pulp. But he'd denied her that pleasure, only to have her try to kill him anyway. Her burning blue eyes were the last thing he remembered. Until the water and the gators. Nothing in between.

Fargo leaned back on his elbows. Nannine had said he'd been there for two days. Probably two more had passed between the time he'd been thrown into the bayou and when she'd found him. Four days wiped away, he grunted. He'd find that big house again, he decided. He had a score to settle with a little blond bitch with burning blue eyes.

His thoughts slid away as he saw Nannine appear in a narrow, double-ended, sharp-prowed little boat. She paddled skillfully with a single, short-handled paddle. "The craft of the bayou, Fargo," she called out. "The pirogue." She brought the little boat to the dock with one quick, deft motion and held up a half-dozen sunfish tied together in a small net. "Dinner," she said, and tossed the catch on the dock. She moored the pirogue to a wooden protrusion alongside the dock and swung from the craft with a motion so quick and graceful it allowed him only a glimpse of long, coffee-and-milk thighs. She took the fish into the cabin and returned to stretch out on her side along the warped boards, and a smile toyed with her lips as she surveyed him.

"I liked you better *tout nu,*" she said. "You have such a marvelous body, so strong, so beautiful to see. And to touch," she added.

"I'm sure you have lots of young bodies to touch, Nannine," Fargo said.

"*Pah!*" she said derisively, and made a face. "Not

27

like yours. Here in the bayous they are either very young boys, old men, or fools who have lost fingers, hands, arms, and feet trying to prove they can catch the big gators alone." She changed moods with dazzling speed as she let a smile wipe away her derisiveness, her black eyes dancing with very female wisdom. "You have come here and I found you. There is a reason. Here in the bayou we believe such things happen because they are meant to happen," she said.

"When you found me, did you see any sign of a horse? An Ovaro pinto, white in the middle, fore, and hind quarters, the rest as black as your hair?" he asked.

"A horse, here in the bayou?" Nannine giggled.

Fargo's lips tightened firmly at her answer. "I thought maybe you'd seen or heard something about a horse," he said.

"I never leave the bayous," Nannine said. "But Jean or Christophe may have heard something at the market. I will ask them."

"Please," Fargo said. "Then you wouldn't know anything about a big house with white columns and arched windows, either?"

She shook her head, turned onto her back, and lifted her knees. The shift slid down to reveal the smooth thighs. She had a way of making even the simplest motion into quicksilver provocativeness, but not with calculation, he decided. A free-spirited, natural grace governed her ways, its own kind of sensuousness. He made a silent wager that there was nothing but her under the tattered shift.

In her high-planed, strong face he could trace the lines of her ancestry—French settlers, black slave stock, and Indian, probably Choctaw or Natchez. In Nannine the result was one of striking loveliness all encased in the warm, glowing sepia tones of her skin. He saw tiny glints of amusement in the black eyes that studied him. "You think you are well enough to leave now?" she asked.

"I feel almost myself, thanks to you," he agreed.

"You do not come from anywhere near here, Fargo. You come from a place of big mountains and much space," she said.

"How do you know that?" He laughed.

"The big spaces are in your eyes, in the way they look far away as the hawk sees. And the mountains are in your face and body, the strongness of rock, the tallness of great peaks," she answered. "Why do you come here, Fargo?" she asked abruptly.

"I was told there is trouble here, bad trouble. I was sent to meet someone in St. Lucifer," he told her.

"Ah, St. Lucifer, I have heard of it. It is not so very far from here, but it is not in the bayou country. I think you go downland to find it," Nannine said.

"Can you take me out of the bayou, Nannine?" Fargo asked, and he caught the flicker of disappointment that touched her face.

"*Oui*, I can do that. But I think you need to rest longer here," she said.

"And I think you just want company." He laughed, and she looked away with the trace of a pout in the high-planed face. "I can come back maybe when I've finished. You show me the way out, and I'll find my way back in. I am called the Trailsman by some."

She studied him for a long moment. "Maybe," she said, and swung to her feet with a quick, graceful movement as she sent a dazzling smile his way. "Let me now show you my bayous," she said, and extended her hand.

He took it, pulled himself up, and she led him into the pirogue. He barely fit into the narrow little craft as he folded himself in behind her. The sides of her round little rear pressed against his legs, warm and soft through the thin shift. Nannine sent the pirogue through the green, still waters with skillful ease. They headed down one of the bayous where the big cypresses seemed ghostlike as they rose from the water.

Fargo's eyes swept the watery avenue and saw the big alligators as they surfaced, sank down again, or just lay partly submerged like unmoving logs. He also noted two water moccasins move through the saw grass at the bank and slide into the water. Nannine chattered proudly in tour-guide fashion as she paddled the pirogue with deft ease, rattling off names of trees he had never heard of before; poison-wood, gumbo-limbo.

"Spider lilies," she said, pointing to a nest of white blossoms with long, spikelike white projections radiating from each bloom.

He saw a large bird—delicate for its size—with a long, thin, curving neck, the long, plumed wingtips of the egret unmistakable.

"Aigrette," Nannine sang out, then pointed to a furry, pepper-and-salt-colored creature clinging to the bark of a cypress. "Mangrove fox squirrel," she explained.

He saw movement near the base of the tree and watched a diamondback rattler slide through the saw grass, dip into the water, and vanish.

Nannine steered the pirogue down another bayou at the right and turned down still another that interconnected. The bayous formed a series of waterways that branched off from one another, mysterious avenues of exotic smells of hyacinth and mimosa blended together. She paddled the craft lazily through the still water. He noticed a pair of particularly huge cypresses rise up from the water to come together and form an arch covered with thick, hanging moss and heavy vines. The entranceway beckoned with mystery. But when Nannine spotted the veiled archway, she swung the pirogue around with sudden sharpness and dug her paddle into the water.

"Wait. Go on through. It looks interesting," Fargo called out.

"No," she said, and turned to cast a severe glance at him.

"Why not?" He frowned.

"No one goes in there. It is a very bad place. *Le diable*, the devil, lives there," Nannine said gravely.

"How do you know?" Fargo prodded.

"Anyone goes through there never come out. It has happened before," she said. "And sometimes at night, even from here, there is strange singing and sometimes screams. *Musique diabolique.*"

Fargo glanced back at the dark entranceway formed by the two huge cypresses and its curtain of hanging moss. He wondered about old folk tales—of natural occurrences given unnatural meanings by the imagination of minds already steeped in mysticism.

As soon as they had moved away from the dark archway, Nannine quickly became her bright, chattery self as she headed the pirogue down still another bayou where masses of green-backed tree frogs clung to the thick vines and tree-trunk bottoms.

"What do you think of my bayous, Fargo? *Magnifique*, no?" she tossed at him as she let the little craft sail on of itself.

"It is," he agreed. "But you have all this water and you can't swim in it without worrying about a gator, a water moccasin, or a big snapper."

"There are places," she said with a secret little smile. "I can show you."

31

He hadn't chance to answer as a shout cut through the still air and he saw Nannine spin around in the little craft as another pirogue shot into sight from a side bayou. He saw the small boy wearing only shorts frantically paddle toward them.

"Nannine, Nannine, come quick, it's Christophe," the boy called. Nannine swung the pirogue in a tight circle and came abreast of the other boat. "He is hurt. He tried to catch a big tortue and fell. Big splash and the gators come at once. One catch him on the leg," the boy said.

"Mon Dieu." Nannine swung the pirgoue after Jean, who began to paddle away furiously.

"I help him reach a cypress root but he cannot hang on long," the boy called over his shoulder as he sent the little craft through the water with skill and speed.

Nannine paddled with matching skill, and as she sent the boat around a bend in the waterway, Fargo saw the youth clinging to the smooth base of a cypress. Christophe clung to a thick vine with both hands, a red gash along the side of his young leg. The pain in the boy's face showed that he was close to the end of his strength. Fargo watched the water that flowed around the tree, which was roiled now with a half-dozen gray shapes that swam back and forth under the boy clinging to the vine. As they watched, one big alligator halted and opened its tremendous jaws, as if inviting his victim to fall into his waiting teeth. Fargo heard Nannine's voice, hardly more than a whisper.

"It is impossible. Christophe will have to drop into the water before we can pull him into the pirogue," she said. "But the gators will have him first. We cannot even get close to him. They will turn us over. It is hopeless."

Christophe's voice cut into Fargo's racing thoughts. "Nannine, my hands, they are slipping," the boy cried out.

"Bring the boat around to the back of the tree so we face that big gator with its mouth open," Fargo ordered.

"What are you thinking?" Nannine said, but quickly steered the pirogue around the circle of alligators.

"I'm guessing they'll act the way a wolf pack acts," Fargo said. "When I say so, tell Christophe to drop. We go in at the same time."

As the pirogue circled and slowed, Fargo saw the big gator close its jaws, make a half-circle in the water, and return to the same spot. Fargo drew his Colt, rested one elbow on the gunwale of the boat, and waited. It was a wait of only moments as the big gator hissed, a sound as loud as a hundred steaming kettles. It opened its huge jaws again to wait with a display of deadly patience.

Fargo sighted down the barrel of the Colt into the gaping mouth, aimed between the double rows of jagged teeth, and pressed the trigger. In an instant, three bullets smashed into the reptile's wide throat, and an explosion of blood, bone, and tissue cascaded out of the giant reptile's mouth. The beast emitted a hissing roar and spun in the water, thrashing furiously as his massive tail slammed hard into the water.

In seconds the water had turned red, and Fargo watched the other alligators close in on the wounded one. In a wolf-pack attack, they began to tear at him with their terrible jaws.

"Now," Fargo shouted to Nannine.

"*Lachez prise*," Nannine shouted. "Let go, Christophe." She dug her paddle into the water and

33

sent the pirogue slicing forward as little Jean did the same with his boat.

Fargo watched Christophe drop into the water, which now churned with the fury of the alligators attacking the wounded one. Fargo dived into the water at a forty-five-degree angle and surfaced only a few yards from the boy. Jean's pirogue reached Christophe first, and Fargo got his arms under the injured boy and half-lifted, half-pushed him into the boat. He cast a glance at the gators and saw one big gray body turn and start toward them. "Get out of here," he ordered Jean, and the boy began to paddle with frantic haste.

The alligator moved through the water with astonishing speed as Nannine brought her pirogue around, and Fargo saw the animal's beady little eyes glittering. The gator began to open his mouth in anticipation, and Fargo cast a glance behind him at Nannine. She had the pirogue there for him, but there was no time to lift himself in as the gator closed in with too much speed. Fargo turned, treaded water as he watched the huge jaws open wider, the jagged, awesome teeth growing into terrifying size. He held a second longer and dived just as the alligator attacked, and he heard the sound of the huge jaws snapping together. He whirled underwater in time to see the big reptile come under Nannine's pirogue to send the little craft up and over.

Fargo surfaced as Nannine screamed and fell backward with the pirogue. The alligator's watery momentum carried it on, and it took the animal a moment to use its big tail to turn. Nannine had grasped the side of the pirogue to turn the craft right side up, and Fargo saw the gator start for her. He dived under her, came up on the underside of the gator, and wrapped his arms around the big reptile's

34

body. The roughness of its back hide dug at the flesh of his arms, but he pressed himself to the comparatively smooth underside. He clung there as the gator turned at once, dived, spun as it tried to shake away this unexpected attacker. Fargo held on as long as he dared, and when it seemed his lungs were ready to burst, he let go and struck out for the surface.

He saw the gator still spinning, still rolling underwater, not yet aware that it had lost the object clinging to it. But it would realize it in a few moments, Fargo knew, and he burst onto the surface of the water to see that Nannine had the pirogue righted and the paddle in hand only a yard away.

She turned the craft toward him as he struck out for it, and she helped pull him in. He collapsed into the boat and turned to see the alligator surface, spin in the water, twisting to find its attacker again. But Nannine had the pirogue moving swiftly through the water, and Fargo drew a deep sigh as they left the scene behind.

"Damn, I'll take a buffalo stampede any day," he muttered, pulling himself into a sitting position and stretching his long legs out alongside Nannine as they came in sight of Jean in the other pirogue. The boy had slowed, and Nannine caught up to him quickly.

"Go right to Doctor Duvallier. I'll fetch Mama Tonton," she said, and Jean nodded as he sent the boat down one of the side waterways. The older boy was alert enough to wave, Fargo saw as Nannine continued on down the bayou. She cast a grave glance at him as she paddled. "You have saved Christophe's life. Mine, too," she said.

"That makes us even." He shrugged.

"We will talk more later," Nannine said.

"Where's the doctor?" Fargo asked.

"Near the marketplace. A distance, but Christophe will make it. He is young and strong. I will leave you at the cabin. It is on the way," Nannine said.

"Mama Ton-ton helps the doctor?" Fargo asked.

"Her medicine is of the spirit," Nannine answered. "His is of the body."

Fargo nodded, and took in all that the answer implied. It seemed hardly minutes when the cabin came into view, and Nannine brought the pirogue against the dock.

"I will be back soon," she said as he swung himself from the boat and watched her send the craft slicing through the water like a giant knife.

He shed wet clothes, spread everything on the boards for the sun to dry, including his naked self as he stretched out on the warm wood. He lay quietly, thoughts sliding through his mind.

The bayou was certainly a deceptive place, he concluded. It masked its dangers with a languorous beauty. Even its stillness was not really still, he realized. Even as he lay in what seemed a silent, sweet-scented world, he heard the distant grunt of a gator, the soft, plopping sounds of leopard frogs jumping into the water from hyacinth beds, the soft swoosh of an egret taking off, and the unsteady hum of a myriad insects. The bayou was a place made for strange imaginings and tales of the devil.

He turned on his stomach and let the sun dry his back. He dozed off, and when he woke, he and his clothes were bone-dry. The air had grown thick as well as hot, and he donned only trousers and lay back. He had to have Nannine guide him out of the bayous, he reminded himself. Too much time had already been lost, and he still had a score to settle with the little blond sadist. He worried about the

Ovaro, too. There'd be no end of people wanting to get their hands on him.

The growing feeling of anxiousness continued to wear at him, and he finally sat up to see the day had begun to drift toward night. The bayou seemed to welcome night as it began to close in on itself with long, twisting shadows. He scanned the moss-hung shores of the waterways as the heavy vines cast tortuous shadows of their own, and he realized how easy it would be for someone who knew the bayous to make his way completely unseen. He was still peering at the darkening shapes when the pirogue appeared, Nannine at the paddle.

She brought the craft to the dock, took his hand, and stepped out. "He will be all right," she said, answering the question in his eyes. "The gash was made by the gator's tail not its teeth. They can cut you bad with that hide of theirs." She led him into the almost dark cabin, released his hand only to light the candle and bring an earthenware jug out from a corner of the room. She pulled the cork and offered the jug to him. "Bayou magic." She smiled. "Especially fine."

He put the jug to his lips and swallowed. At first he thought a tongue of flame had gone down his throat, but a sweet warmth followed instantly, unlike anything he had ever tasted. Nannine took the jug, drew a deep swallow, and followed with a rush of breath and a pleased little giggle. The one swallow he'd taken curled through him, and he felt the warm kick of it.

"It is made in charred casks from the West Indies," she told him as she put the jug down. "One sip is usually enough." She smiled, and her black eyes danced.

"I can believe it," Fargo said.

Nannine came toward him, her face suddenly grave. "You are a brave man, Fargo. Brave and strong. My brothers and I, all my family, we bow to you."

"No need for that. Things happen, and you do what has to be done," he told her.

"We believe here in the bayou that to be close to the brave is to take on some of their bravery," she said, and he saw her arms reach up, slide around his neck. Her lips pressed against his mouth, firm and warm, and he felt her tongue dart out, return to safety at once. Her hands pressed against his bare chest, moved lightly down to his waist and back up to cover both his nipples.

"I do not need that reason, though," she said, and her mouth edged a very private smile. She stepped back, lifted her arms high, and with one, quick motion whisked the tattered shift off to stand absolutely naked before him. Naked and beautiful, he saw in admiration as his eyes took in the lithe, coffee-with-milk body. Her breasts curved upward with saucy impudence, little dark-brown nipples on pink-brown circles, and below, her ribcage showed the outline of ribs and moved down to a thimble-sized waist. Her hips flared, though, in sudden womanliness, and her belly lay flat above the tangled, thick nap, as jet-black as the long hair on her head. Her legs were long, slender stalks, all of her forming a symphony of sepia sensuousness.

Her hands reached out, unbuttoned the waist of his trousers, pushed, and the garment fell to the floor. He pulled off his drawers as he felt himself responding to the beauty of her. She fell to her knees on the mattress, her arms raised to him. He sank down atop her as she went back and felt the smooth, skin fiery warm against his. His powerful maleness slapped against her tangled black nap, and he heard her gasp out in

38

pleasure. Nannine's arms came around his neck, pulled his face down to her breasts. He took one lovely sepia mound into his mouth, pulled gently on it, and felt the tiny nipple enlarge, growing firm under his tongue.

"Oh, yes, yes . . . *oui, oui*. So *magnifique*," Nannine gasped out as her hand came to press the bottom of one breast upward so all of it could enter his mouth. "Aaaah, yes. *Oui* . . . oh, *oui*," she cried out as he sucked, pulled, caressed her breasts. He felt her lean form come hard against him, clinging to him as she moved her legs up and down over his thighs. "Yes, Fargo. Oh, good, good, *bon, bon*," she murmured.

She fell back on the mattress and he went with her, his hands moving down the smooth body. Nannine arched her back, pressed the thick, black curly mat against him, and he let his fingers dig into its luxurious tangle. Nannine made a tiny sound, almost like a giggle. A little cry of undeniable pleasure followed, and he moved down to stroke the insides of the slender, smooth thighs as he caressed the upturned breasts with his lips. Nannine's legs fell open, and her hand came down and closed over his, pressing him to her warm moistness.

"Please. Oh, yes, big Fargo . . . so very big Fargo," he heard her murmur, and she wrapped her legs around him in one quick motion as she arched her slender back. He found her dark entranceway, pushed into her, and heard her cry of pleasure. Nannine's legs clamped hard around him and she began to move with a quick, harsh motion, quivering with each push of her body as a steel-wire tension seemed to seize her.

"Faster, faster," Nannine cried out between her gasps of delight. "Oh, yes, please faster." Her hands moved up and down his body, then halted to dig into his shoulders as she thrust upward to match his increasing speed. Her dark tangle grew moist, and he felt a thin coating of perspiration on her body. She smelled wonderfully dark and sexual, and he felt himself delighting in his powerful thrusts in a new way, a wild, strange excitement inside him. It was Nannine, he realized, sweeping him up with the unvarnished sexuality of her desire. It was body communicating itself to body, flesh answering flesh, and he found himself half-laughing with her as she squealed and made little chortling sounds with every sensation that swept through her. "Yes, yes, oh, *oui, oui*," she cried out, mixing languages as one, clutching him to her with increasing fervor.

Her lifting, pushing little pelvis matched his every thrust until he felt the tight legs around him suddenly grow even tighter. "Fargo, oh, *mon Dieu*, now," Nannine gasped, and her back arched. He moved hard inside her as he felt her orgasm sweep through her. She screamed, and the scream became a wild cry of delight. "*Merveilleux . . . merveilleux*," she gasped out between cries, and he stroked her throughout the climax until she fell back on the mattress and her breath came in short, hard gasps.

"Enough . . . oh, *mon Dieu . . . ça suffit*," she said breathlessly, but there was no protest in her voice, only satiated contentment. The thin coating of perspiration made her sepia skin shine with a luxuriant beauty, and he lay down beside her. She turned to him, curled up in his arms, and slept almost instantly. He smiled, let his own eyes close, and slept beside her as the scent of magnolia drifted through the open doorway of the little cabin.

He woke when he felt her move. He opened his eyes and knew they had slept for at least an hour, perhaps two. Nannine rose, flashed a contented smile at him. "I am hungry. I will fix the dinner. You stay, rest more," she said.

She left the shift on the floor and walked naked across the room. He watched her slender, coffee-and-milk body move with consummate, natural grace as she prepared the sunfish and put them into a skillet over the small cooking area made of stones. The fish took only a few minutes to fry and she brought them on a large, earthenware platter, handed him a tin fork, and kept one for herself. With sips from the jug of bayou bourbon, the meal was fit for a king, and he felt like one in the luxury of his harem as Nannine, beautifully naked, sat across from him. He watched the beautiful way in which the saucy breasts dipped as she moved, rose up to point upward, swung together when she took the plate back and swept up little crumbs of food.

Childlike, he murmured silently as he watched her. There was an ingenuous simplicity and utter naturalness to her that gave her sexuality a kind of exhilirating freedom.

She returned to sit cross-legged in front of him. "I almost forgot, Jean told me there was talk at the market of a great horse some men were trying to catch," she said.

"My Ovaro. I must leave, come morning," he said.

Her little shrug was made of resignation. "The morning will come. Tonight is here," she said as she leaned forward and rose to her knees, wrapped her arms around his neck, the brown tips of her upturned breasts touching his chest.

"So it is," he agreed, and she laughed as he leaned back and pulled her down on top of him. She lay over him and rubbed the tangly black nap up and down against his organ, letting the sensation speed his

41

response. As he felt himself thicken, rise, throb, she lifted herself, brought her legs against him, and pushed over him with her already moist darkness. Nannine cried out in glee. She threw back her head, and her black hair hung low and long enough to touch his thighs. She shook the luxuriant locks and laughed as he rolled her onto her back, staying inside her. Her passion was made of pure, simple delight, Fargo saw, her lovemaking an exercise in uncomplicated joy.

"More, Fargo, more, more, more." She half-laughed, half-gasped as she rose up with his every push forward. She almost cried out when he drew back, and laughed in utter pleasure as he came forward. Nannine generated her own special excitement, and once again as she pushed and rose, pushed and rose, her energy brought the thin coating of perspiration to her body and she virtually shone in the flickering candlelight. He pressed himself down over her smooth, moist skin and felt the silken touch of her, gathered one coffee-and-milk breast into his mouth as she cried out in delight. He heard her call to him again in a breathless command.

"Faster, oh, oh, faster." He responded as he felt her dark softness begin to tighten around him. Nannine twisted to one side as she arched her back, as though she could wring every last bit of esctasy out of her body. "Aaaaaaaah," she cried, her voice drifting into a reluctant sigh as she fell back and lay still. He stayed in her for a while, then slipped down beside her, and she curled against him again and was asleep in moments.

He slept beside her, and the deep of the night finally slid into the pink gray of dawn. Fargo woke as the filtered sun crept into the cabin. He rose and went outside to wash with the warm water that lapped the dockside. Nannine still slept. He had half-dressed when he looked up to see her standing in the doorway. Her beautiful nakedness seemed totally in place here in this strange exotic world. "You going to lead me out of here like that?" He smiled.

She half-pouted, then turned into the cabin as he finished dressing. She ran past him still naked, as he started inside, and he frowned in alarm as she dived into the water. She disappeared, surfaced, shook herself, and climbed onto the dock. She had done it all in seconds and she stretched in the morning sun, her skin glistening with tiny droplets of water.

"You're making it damn hard for me to leave, aren't you?" Fargo grunted.

Her laugh was quick. "I'm making it easy for you to come back," she said. She strode past him into the cabin, brushed her hair vigorously, and dried herself with a towel as he watched. The beauty of her seared into his mind. Finally she picked up the shift, wriggled into it almost disdainfully, and strode from the cabin.

"Follow me," she said, and made her way behind the cabin where a mangrove thicket grew in dense profusion. He felt the softness of the ground at once and stayed on Nannine's heels as she picked her way between red mangroves. He took note of a trio of bent cypresses where she made a turn left and moved close to a single row of pond cypress mixed in with black willow. She stayed close to the trees and turned left again where a swamp of fungus-covered dead tree stumps stretched to the right. He made a mental note of the trail mark.

He felt the ground grow firmer under his steps as Nannine moved up a slope and halted. He came up to her and saw the green flatland where the trees were mostly weeping willows. A tall rock with a wide willow on each side of it marked the spot, and he stored that in his mind.

"There, the back country," Nannine said as she stayed inside the last of the pond cypresses. "Go straight maybe a mile, then south, and you will come around to the marketplace in time, I am told. You can ask more there," she told him.

"Did they bring me in this way?" Fargo asked.

Nannine shrugged. "There are other ways into the bayous. I know this one because it is closest to the cabin," she answered.

He turned to her, took her face in his hands. "Maybe I can come back, Nannine," he said.

"Try hard, Fargo. I would like it," she said. "I will be waiting." She reached up on her toes and kissed him, her lips lingering for a moment. Suddenly she whirled away and was gone, flitting through the cypresses with the swiftness of a swallow.

Nannine, he murmured silently, and promised himself he'd try to return. She was not to be quickly forgotten. But neither was that pretty-faced, blond bitch.

His eyes grew cold as he turned and struck out across the thick carpet of grass.

3

The tall, long-legged man moved across the thick bluegrass with a long, loping gait, not unlike that of a timber wolf. It was a gait he had mastered long ago, and it devoured distance and time while expending a minimum of energy. After he had gone a mile or so, Fargo turned as Nannine had instructed, and headed south. The Louisiana back country was lush with plenty of bluegrass, lamb's-quarter goosefoot, weeping willow, black ash, and honey locust, he took note. The land rose in small inclines, hardly large enough to be termed hills, and he soon found a road that carried wagon tracks.

He knelt down and read the tracks the way other men read books. The wagon tracks were mostly of donkey carts and small berry wagons. It was the road to the market, he was certain, and he rose and returned to his long, loping gait. He had traveled another mile, running along the bottom of a hilly rise, when he heard the shouts from the other side of the low hill, men's voices raised in frustration and anger.

"He's getting away, again," one voice shouted.

"Get on the other side of him, dammit," another called out.

Fargo whirled, and his heels dug into the ground as

he raced up the low hill to reach the top. He peered down at the scene below, and his eyes found the Ovaro first, the horse racing from three riders swinging lariats. As he watched, two of the riders started to converge on the Ovaro, and the horse let them come in closer. Fargo felt a smile edge his lips. The two riders half-rose in their saddles as they closed, lariats poised, and Fargo saw the Ovaro had deliberately slowed to let his pursuers converge.

"We got him, Harry," one of the men yelled, and the moment he did, the Ovaro braked, pushed powerful fore and hind legs out stiffly, and the two riders overshot him by yards, their lariats roping only air. The Ovaro spun and easily outran the third man.

Fargo whistled, and the magnificent horse turned in a wide circle. He whistled again as he started to run down the hill, and this time the horse spotted him. The Ovaro met him halfway down the hill and reared into the air with a neigh of joyful recognition.

"Good boy, easy now," Fargo said as the big mount crashed his hooves down only inches from him. He reached out, took the hanging reins, and drew the horse in a tight circle as he patted the sleek black neck. The horse nuzzled him, and he stroked the velvet snout. He knelt down and ran his hands expertly over the horse's legs. He rubbed slowly down along the forelegs, examining knee, fetlock, pastern, the cannon bone. He was doing the same with the hind legs when the three horsemen drew up. Two were young boys; the third, a lean man with graying hair and gray eyes, looked at the Ovaro with the gaze of an experienced horseman. "I'll be dammed," he muttered. "It's plain you know that horse, mister."

"I should. He's mine," Fargo said. "Name's Fargo. Skye Fargo."

"I'm Jack Culligan. We've been trying to catch him

for days. He's not only fast; he's smart," the man said. "How'd you lose him?"

Fargo weighed words before answering and decided to be careful. Enough strange things had happened already to dictate prudence. "A storm, some days back, real bad," he said.

The man nodded. "Yes, it sure was," he agreed.

"Took a fall, hit my head on a rock, and lost him," Fargo said.

Jack Culligan eyed him. "You're not from around here," he said.

"No, I'm from the plains country out West," Fargo said.

The man pushed his hat back on his head and drew a deep sigh. "I wonder if you'd do us a mighty big favor," he said. "We work for Gail Bonnard. She saw your horse, and she's had us trying to catch him ever since. Gail Bonnard doesn't like not getting what she wants. When we tell her about your coming along, she's going to think we just lost the horse and came up with that story."

"You want me to back it up in person," Fargo said, and the man nodded.

"It could cost us our jobs otherwise," he said.

"I'll do it. Might need a favor sometime before I leave here." Fargo smiled.

"We'll remember this, Fargo," the man said. "The Bonnard place is across from the bayous. Turn north to a road with three forks and take the right fork. You can't miss the place. Everybody knows the Bonnards around here."

"I'll stop by tonight. Right now I've got to go to St. Lucifer and find a man named Joe Alcott," Fargo said.

"Joe Alcott? He puts out the county paper. He's got

his press in the center of town," Culligan said as he turned his horse. "Thanks, again."

Fargo nodded, and the three men rode away as he swung up onto the Ovaro. He smiled as he settled into the saddle. "Feels like coming home," he murmured as he stroked the powerful neck and sent the horse into a trot. He returned to the road and finally saw the buildings of the town come into view.

St. Lucifer wasn't a large town, he reckoned. It had the usual dance hall and saloon, but many of the buildings had a special Louisiana flavor, small wrought-iron fences, railings, and slanted roofs. He reached the center of the town and spotted the square window in a low-roofed building, the name in gold on the glass. THE EXPRESS, he read and dismounted in front of the building.

He walked into the office, and a thin-faced man looked up from where he was setting a font of type on a printing press. He wore a green eyeshade pushed up and a pair of denim coveralls. "Joe Alcott?" Fargo asked.

"It is," the man said as he put down the type and came forward. He had a gentle face, Fargo noted, not a hard line in it, with sad gray eyes and a quietness about him. He was a man plainly more at home with Shakespeare than six-guns.

"Ned Simmons said you'd be expecting me. Name's Fargo," the Trailsman said, and saw the man's eyes widen.

"Yes, of course," Joe Alcott replied and extended his hand. "Sit down please," the man offered, and pushed proofsheets onto the floor to clear a chair in front of a battered wooden desk. Fargo eased himself onto the chair, and Joe Alcott found space on a corner of the desk to perch his thin frame. "No problems getting here, I hope," the man said.

"Not until about five days ago," Fargo said. As Alcott frowned, he told him of the storm, the house, how he was nearly killed, and about Nannine. When he had finished, the man's frown dug deep lines into his brow.

"Good God, that's a strange piece of business," the man muttered. "There are enough old houses around, but I don't know of one with a pretty blonde and a giant hulk in it. As for the bayou people, they keep pretty much to themselves."

"I'll do some looking, I promise you that," Fargo muttered grimly.

"You've more than that to look for, Fargo," Joe Alcott said. "Another three girls disappeared."

"When?" Fargo asked.

"About two weeks ago," Alcott said as he swung from the desk and sat down on a swivel chair behind it. He opened a drawer, pulled out a roll of bills, and pushed them at Fargo. "The pay Ned Simmons sent for you," he said.

"Anyone know anything about the last three girls?" Fargo asked as he pocketed the bills.

"They were on their way by coach from New Orleans," Alcott said. "The driver was left dead."

"I take it somebody looked for them," Fargo commented.

"Ray Guiness. He's the county sheriff," Alcott answered. "But Ray's in over his head on this, and he's way past his best years."

"Suppose you fill me in from the beginning," Fargo said, and leaned back in his chair.

"Girls started disappearing a few years back. But only once in a while. Then it got to be a steady thing, every few months, and now they're vanishing almost every month. Ned Simmons' daughter and my niece disappeared a little over a month ago. They and two other young women were traveling up the Calla-hatchie River on a small barge. The Callahatchie is winding and narrow. The barge was found, the barge tender on it with his neck broken. Most times, girls have disappeared from stagecoaches or private carriages. Nobody with them is ever found alive to talk."

"You run the local newspaper. You hear more than most folks, but nothing on this? No ransom notes, no explanations of any kind?" Fargo questioned.

"Only theories. The most likely one is that they're being taken for the slave trade across the Mexican border. Down there they're either sold to private parties or put into the whorehouses," Alcott said, and Fargo saw the disgust and pain flood his face.

"From what you've told me, there might be another attack pretty damn soon. Maybe we can stop this one," Fargo said.

"If we knew who was coming on what stage or carriage," the man answered. "Trouble is, we don't—not until we find a dead coachman or relatives start asking why their daughter didn't arrive."

"How do the attackers know?"

"I don't think they do. Somehow they wait and watch," Alcott said.

"What do you mean 'somehow'?" Fargo frowned.

"I mean, most of this area is low brush, especially along the roads It'd be damn hard for a man to hide out unseen, much less a horse and rider," Joe Alcott said.

"And there has to be more than one of them," Fargo thought aloud.

Alcott nodded gravely. "Roy Guiness has had patrols ride every road, and they've never seen a soul. They're phantoms nobody sees before, during, or after."

"I don't put much store in phantoms," Fargo said,

and gave voice to the thoughts that took shape in his mind. "If these girls are kidnapped to be sold in Mexico, they've got to be taken someplace first, then somewhere else to be held until the buyers arrive. That means a hiding place, a house, a cabin, a cave. Something real, that's for sure. It can't be done out of thin air. I'll have to find it."

"God, I hope you can, Fargo. Anything you want me to do, you just tell me," Alcott said.

"Good enough. Meanwhile, I'm going to have a look around for myself. I want to ride those main roads," Fargo said.

"Go west out of town. There are only two roads, and the Callahatchie's just beyond the second one," Allcott said as Fargo rose and started for the door. Allcott slid from the desk and followed the big man outside, where his eyes took in the Ovaro. "Magnificent," he said. "Beauty and power."

"I'll be back tomorrow," Fargo said. "I'm stopping at the Bonnard place tonight."

"The Bonnards?" Joe Alcott echoed as surprise flooded his tired face. "You move into high society real quick, Fargo."

"Who are the Bonnards?" Fargo asked.

"They run Thurmond Parish, which is where you are. A parish is what you'd call a county out West. Old man Bonnard's dead now, but Gail and her brother run the family holdings—cotton, lumber, potatoes, sugarcane, pecans, and just about everything else the state produces. Needless to say, they're also leaders of Louisiana high society. How do you come to be stopping at their place?" Alcott queried.

"Just doing their foreman a favor." Fargo laughed as he swung onto the Ovaro. He turned the horse down the main street and rode out of town past the balance of St. Lucifer's ornamented houses. He rode west, found the two roads and the narrow, winding river, then sent the Ovaro up and down both roads and along the riverbank for some five miles in both directions. Joe Alcott had indeed been right about the roadside cover, he noted. The low brush hardly afforded a place for a man to hide even on foot, and he rode into the back country where the hills were gentle. There was better tree cover there, but they were too far back to see the roads. He made a wide circle and took in rocks, trees, anything unusual enough to act as a landmark.

He came across a half-dozen farmhouses and halted at each. He rode away certain they held no kidnapped young women, not with herds of youngsters running about. He also found himself searching for a big house with arched windows and white columns across the entrance.

He had crested a low hill when he saw a big, ramshackle house half-hidden in a patch of buckthorns. It wasn't the house out of the storm, but he dismounted and walked to the front door, where ivy all but obscured the entrance.

Hidden behind the buckthorn, the house'd be a perfect stopping-off place to bring kidnapped young women, Fargo thought as he pushed against the front door. The door swung open at once, and Fargo's hand rested on the butt of the Colt at his hip as he stepped inside. His glance swept past the broken furniture and the peeling wallpaper of the room to scan the dust-covered floor. He uttered a grim sound as he took his hand from the gun. No one had brought anyone here to hide away. The dust was undisturbed, cobwebs covering the doorways unbroken. Just to be sure, he checked the rest of the house, but it was only more of the same untouched, undisturbed dust. He returned to his horse as the day drew to a close, the lavender dusk turning to blackness as the night pushed itself across the land.

He grimaced as he rode north. An uneasy apprehension rode with him, nothing he could give form or shape to yet, but he had a foreboding that something more than the greed of unscrupulous men lay at the heart of this search. Something dark and sinister lay curled and waiting, he felt with increasing uneasiness. Perhaps it was the foreboding of the bayous that still clung to him, he told himself, and he forced aside the feeling. He put the Ovaro into a trot, found the road with the three forks, and turned north at the first fork. The quarter moon let only dark shadows move through the night until he saw a soft glow of light and hurried the horse forward.

The big house came into view, all the rooms lighted, and he heard the faint sound of music. The murmur of voices and laughter reached his ears as he drew closer. He guided the horse around to the front of the house, where he saw phaetons, bretts, stanhopes, victorias, and landaulets parked along with a variety of smaller carriages. His gaze went on to the big house. He drew his breath in sharply and frowned as he reined the horse to an abrupt halt. He stared open-mouthed and heard his murmured oath. "Goddamn," he swore in astonishment as he continued to stare at the tall white columns, the terraced balcony over the front door, and the tall, arched windows on either side. A wooden sign on a post bore the name DARK WILLOWS.

He swung to the ground with his eyes still fixed on the house and looped the Ovaro's reins over a wrought-iron hitching post. It was the house in the storm, the very same one, he murmured to himself, everything the same; columns, arched windows, terraced balcony, even the bay windows at the wings.

Everything the same. It wasn't the kind of house that could be duplicated, unless builders copied one another down here. He frowned at the thought as he stepped through the open front door to walk into a foyer. Beyond, he saw the big room filled with swirling dancers, women in evening gowns, men in formal dress. An elderly black man in a butler's outfit approached him, and Fargo saw him take in the trail clothes he wore.

"Came to see Gail Bonnard," Fargo said, and the butler hesitated. "Tell her the man with the Ovaro is here," he added, and watched the man go into the big room. Fargo followed, halted at the edge of the dancing couples. He took in walls of deep red, a magnificent crystal chandelier, and two white spiral stairways that curved up at the far end of the room. The house was beautiful and gracious, designed with a grandeur that fitted the elegantly clothed merrymakers. Perhaps it wasn't the same house, he found himself wondering. It sure as hell bore no relationship to the dark, silent, forbidding house that had appeared out of the storm. He had to see the cellar, he told himself. That would tell him once and for all, and he felt the thought send a surge of grim anger through him as he found himself looking forward to confronting a pretty blond bitch. He stared at the swirling dancers when a voice cut into his angry thoughts.

"So it's true," the voice said, and he turned to face a tall young woman in a green silk evening gown. She had dark-brown hair hanging to smooth bare shoulders, a thin, patrician nose, and wide-set gray eyes. Her lips were red and full and softly modeled. Her strikingly lovely face contained a hint of imperiousness in it. Creamy white, full breasts rose up over the edge of the square-cut neckline of the gown, and the rest of her figure was hidden behind the ballooned folds below.

"Yes, it's true. The horse is right outside," Fargo said.

The young woman turned and strode to the doorway. She peered outside for a moment and returned to him. He saw her gray eyes move up and down the hard-muscled breadth of his body, linger on the intense, chiseled lines of his face. "You fit," Gail Bonnard commented. "Handsome horse, handsome rider."

"You fit, too," Fargo returned. "Beautiful house, beautiful owner."

Her smile was warm and lovely, glistening white teeth revealed as the red, full lips pulled back. "I confess I had trouble accepting Jack Culligan's story. Thank you for coming by, mister . . . ?" She hesitated.

"Fargo, Skye Fargo," he filled in.

"I hate to accuse someone wrongly, and you've prevented me from doing that," Gail Bonnard said. "Come in and have a drink."

Fargo cast a glance at the elegantly turned out couples. "I'm not dressed for this kind of a party," he said.

"Don't bother about that," she said, and took his arm as she led him through the merrymakers to a long table bearing a huge silver punch bowl and dozens of silver goblets. She filled two of the goblets, handed him one, and raised hers into the air. "Cheers," she said. "And thank you again for coming by."

He took a long draw of the goblet and tasted the bourbon that was at the heart of the punch. "Good, real good," he remarked as his eyes took in Gail Bonnard's dark-haired loveliness. He let his gaze sweep the dancers again and kept his voice casual. "Anyone live here beside you?" he asked.

"Only my brother and the servants. Why?" Gail Bonnard asked quickly.

"Just being curious," Fargo said. "Such a big house and all." He smiled and flicked his eyes over the young women in the big room. There were plenty of blondes, but not the one he sought. He'd recognize her even decked out in party finery, he was certain, and held the frown inside himself. It seemed to be the same house, but nothing else fit. He watched as two men walked toward him, both dressed in black velvet evening jackets. One was tall, neatly trimmed black hair with a little too much oil on it, his good looks spoiled by a disdainful air. The other, shorter, had Gail Bonnard's gray eyes, her patrician nose, her face without any of her strength.

"My brother, Thomas," Gail Bonnard said of the shorter man. "And this is Jeremy Tallant." She took both in as she spoke. "Mr. Skye Fargo. He owns that magnificent Ovaro I wanted so badly."

Her brother's brows lifted. "Then Culligan wasn't making up a story," the young man said.

"I'm afraid not," Fargo said.

"Well, I'm glad for that much," Tom Bonnard said. "From your outfit, I'd say you're from the plains country."

"You'd be right," Fargo agreed, and saw Gail Bonnard's eyes studying him.

"I still want that Ovaro. How about selling him?" she asked. Before Fargo could reply, he heard Jeremy Tallant's voice.

"Oh, come now, Gail, that's really a peasant horse," the man said with a sneer.

"You're wrong, Jeremy," the young woman snapped.

Tom Bonnard's voice cut in. "You'll never get Gail to marry you if you keep disagreeing with her on horses." He laughed.

"I just hate to see her get carried away with herself," Jeremy Tallant said as he flicked a glance at Fargo. "No insult intended, my good man, but I do know horses," he added.

"So do I, cousin," Fargo said, irritated by the man's sneering air. "He's more horse than you'll ever have under you."

Jeremy Tallant's brows lifted, but the disdain stayed in his face. It was a built-in part of the man, Fargo decided. "Is that a challenge?" Jeremy Tallant asked.

"Just a statement of fact," Fargo replied smoothly.

"Why don't you bring him to the meet tomorrow?" the man asked snidely.

"That's not fair," Gail Bonnard cut in, and Fargo saw her eyes flash gray fire at Tallant. "Even an unusual horse can't be expected to stand up against top Thoroughbreds and jumpers," she said.

Tallant ignored her and fastened his eyes on the big man in front of him. "The Thurmond Horse Club is holding its annual meet tomorrow. The main event is a steeplechase race over a most difficult course. Anyone can enter," he said. "Plenty of prizes."

"Sorry," Fargo answered.

Tallant didn't try to hide the disdain in his smile. "Afraid that horse of yours won't hold up to top stock, Fargo?" he taunted.

Fargo kept his face and voice calm. "Maybe. Or maybe I don't need proving or prizes."

"The winner of the steeplechase receives no ordinary prize. He'll have the honor of Gail as his guest for an entire day," Tallant said.

"Not interested," Fargo said, and his eyes met Gail Bonnard's appraising observation.

"I consider that an insult to the lady," Tallant blustered.

Fargo speared the man with eyes suddenly ice blue. "No insult, junior, just not interested," he growled.

"I still say it's an insult," Tallant insisted, and Fargo heard Gail's voice break in.

"I think the prize is too genteel to interest Mr. Fargo," she said, and he saw the little lights of amusement in the gray eyes.

"Something like that," he agreed.

"You'd prefer all night to all day," she said with an amused smile.

"Go to the head of the class," Fargo returned blandly.

"By God, I ought to teach you some manners for a remark like that, Fargo," Jeremy Tallant said stormily.

"Oh, Jeremy, be quiet. I understand Fargo quite well," Gail said. "Where he comes from they don't play little social games."

Fargo's smile broadened. Her remark was double-edged, he knew.

"Well, if you'll all excuse me, I see Don Russ over there, and I want to talk to him," Tom Bonnard sa' l, and strode away. Gail's eyes remained on Fargo as Jeremy Tallant frowned at her.

"Dammit, Gail, sometimes I just don't understand you," he said. "I fail to see why you suffer the company of boors." He spun on his feet and strode away.

Gail's eyes never left his, Fargo noted. "Jeremy has a bad temper," she said.

"I hope he can back it up," Fargo commented.

The young woman's gray eyes continued to dance

with private amusement. "I wish you would come to the meet. It would add a little spice to it," she said.

"You adding any spice to the first prize?" Fargo asked mildly.

Her smile held a moment of amused thoughtfulness. "One never knows," she said. "Think about it. I've guests to see to, but do have another drink."

"Thanks," Fargo said. "I like beautiful houses. Mind if I look around some?"

"Please do," Gail Bonnard said, and swept away, a lovely vision in green silk.

Fargo watched her become involved with other guests, Jeremy Tallant hovering nearby. Then the Trailsman began to edge his way to the hallway beyond the foyer. He paused to let his gaze sweep the crowd again. Most were young and attractive, he saw, the women sending out waves of that special southern combination of charm, beauty and purpose. The men showed the marks of fancy schools and the arrogance of too much money too soon.

Fargo edged himself out of the large, busy room and moved across the foyer to the wide hallway. He peered down the corridor and spotted a narrow doorway halfway down toward the west wing of the house. As he walked toward it, two pretty young women passed nearby. He studied a delicate straight-backed chair against one wall of the hallway until they'd gone.

He moved quickly. When he reached the narrow door, he pulled it open and saw a flight of steps leading downward. He left the door slightly ajar to let in a shaft of light and started down the steps. Halting at the bottom, he let his eyes adjust to the darkness. He espied a kerosene lamp near the bottom step. The little blonde had held a kerosene lamp, he remembered grimly as he lighted it, turning it up just enough to send a soft glow across the cellar. His eyes moved over the wooden crates, the old bedstand, and the two brass-fitted trunks. They had all been in the cellar of the house out of the storm. Yet brass-fitted trunks and old bedstands were probably in every cellar, and he swore silently. He crossed the room to look up at the cellar storm door. It was in the right spot, he grunted as he turned away and scanned the cellar again. Everything seemed right. Everything looked the same, yet he couldn't be a hundred percent sure. All cellars had broken boxes and crates and brass-fitted trunks. "Dammit to hell," he whispered aloud as he strode to the trunk and leaned over to peer behind it. There was no broken shovel handle, and he turned away and swore again as his mind summoned up images.

The battle had ended near the trunk. He remembered that much all too clearly. He had smashed the hulk with the broken shovel handle, torn the side of his temple open. The giant had fallen facedown, blood pouring from his torn temple onto the floor. Fargo raised the lamp higher to spread a larger circle of light, and stared at the floor. There was no sign of blood anywhere, but he saw something else and the frown deepened in his brow. He dropped to one knee and brought the lamp down closer. There was no blood, but a portion of the floor had been unmistakably scrubbed clean. He stared at the irregularly shaped area, two shades lighter than the surrounding floorboards. This was the house, he muttered silently, no longer any question in his mind. The blood had been cleaned away.

Fargo started to rise as he heard footsteps and saw Tom Bonnard halfway down the steps. The man's face wore a frown as he saw the big black-haired figure with the lamp in hand.

"What are you doing down here?" Tom Bonnard asked.

"I like to see the way these big houses are built," Fargo lied calmly. "Your sister told me I could look around."

"I hardly think she meant to go poking about down here," Tom Bonnard snapped. "I just happened to see the cellar door open."

"Sorry, guess I misunderstood," Fargo said as he put the lamp out and followed Tom Bonnard up the cellar stairs. The man was plainly bothered. Too bothered, Fargo decided.

"Gail is busy with our guests. I'll tell her you had to leave," Bonnard said pointedly when they reached the corridor upstairs.

"Do that." Fargo smiled cheerfully and strolled through the foyer to the front door. His smile disappeared when he reached the Ovaro, swung onto the horse, and rode away from the house. He cast a glance backward. It was the same house, he reiterated silently. It was beautifully transformed, brought sparklingly alive, but the same house nonetheless. The frown creased his brow as he rode. None of it fit—not yet, anyway. Certainly Gail Bonnard wasn't the little pretty-faced blonde that had been in the dark, deserted cellar. No amount of transformation could effect that. But Tom Bonnard had been too upset at finding him in the cellar. Perhaps beauty could be as much a mask with houses as with women.

He spotted a honey locust and guided the Ovaro under its thick branches. He swung to the ground and laid out his bedroll. As he undressed and stretched out, he let thoughts take form. He'd find out what more Joe Alcott could tell him about the Bonnards,

61

Fargo mused. And the Thurmond Horse Meet suddenly seemed worth attending.

He closed his eyes and the wind brought the faint scent of gardenia to him as he drifted off to sleep in the warm Louisiana night.

4

The large tent, the brightly colored banners, and the excited crowds marked the scene as Fargo slowly approached. He had wakened early; washed at a stream, and asking directions of a passing berry salesman, found that the Thurmond County Horse Meet was a well-known event. He circled and came up along the rear edge of the crowd that milled about both on foot and on horseback, and paused to watch a three-gaited saddle-horse contest in a large circle. He moved on. He spied a crowd of horses and people at a flat, straight area hung with a banner marked START-ING LINE. Most everyone was turned out in very proper riding habits—bright-red or black riding coats on both the men and the women. He saw Tom Bonnard talking to two young women in dresses, and he steered the Ovaro toward him.

Bonnard looked up, saw him, and his jaw dropped open.

" 'Morning," Fargo said affably.

Tom Bonnard swallowed, found his voice. "I thought you'd said you weren't coming." He frowned.

"Changed my mind." Fargo smiled. "See you around." He moved the Ovaro forward and was aware of the stares his horse and his western garb attracted. He halted near a refreshment stand where two young girls all in pink sold drinks, but his eyes watched Tom Bonnard as the man hurried through the crowd. Fargo saw him rush up to Gail where she waited near the starting-line banner, his face flushed and tense as he spoke to her. The young woman listened and Fargo saw Gail Bonnard's full red lips purse in thought for a moment. Finally she said something to her brother, and he turned away, his face darkened, and pushed his way back through the crowds.

Fargo's eyes returned to Gail. She was dressed in a red riding outfit. He circled the Ovaro behind the tent to come up in front of where she stood beside a dark-sable standardbred, a good-looking horse with the strength of a jumper in his forequarters.

The girl saw him and her smile was one of contained amusement. "You like surprising people, it seems," she said.

"Why not?" He laughed.

The gray eyes studied him thoughtfully. "What made you decide to come?" she asked.

"Kept thinking about the prize," he returned.

"And I think that you've some other reason," Gail Bonnard remarked.

"Maybe." Fargo half-shrugged, and his eyes moved over her outfit, the red riding jacket bulging out beautifully. "You're not just the prize. You're the competition," he said.

"Yes, I am, and I always win. I'm the prize no one's ever won but me." She laughed.

"There's always a first time," Fargo commented.

Her smile was chiding. "I still love your Ovaro, but I hardly think he can compete against our best mounts in this kind of race," Gail said.

A voice cut in and Fargo turned to see Jeremy Tallant striding up, resplendent in red riding jacket, black cap, and black britches.

"By God, this is a surprise. I really thought you had more sense than to show up, old fellow," the man said. "I think I'll enjoy this race more than any I've ever been in."

"Me, too, friend," Fargo said softly, and his eyes went to Gail. "I think I'm allowed to check out the course," he said.

"You are indeed," she agreed. "You'll find it quite difficult, and we go around twice."

He nodded and turned the Ovaro into a trot, heading down the straight section that formed the starting and finishing lines. He followed a wide curve and then the flags that marked the edge of the course as it moved out into open country. Gail hadn't exaggerated. Most of the jumps were natural, but they had put in others and had made some of the natural jumps more difficult by adding extra rails. There were natural stone walls of varying heights, plenty of water jumps, high open ditches, thick brush obstacles, chicken-coop jumps, three-pole hogbacks, post-and-rail jumps, and two shallow riverbeds to cross before the course wound its way back to the finish line.

Fargo rode slowly, his eyes taking in each obstacle. The mounts he had seen gathered were all jumpers and hunters—Thoroughbreds, standardbreds, Arabians, and a few saddlebreds. All were horses that could jump well, run fast, and were used to exhibition jumping. This course was designed to take its toll and wear down the contestants.

Fargo smiled grimly as he returned to the starting line, where Gail and the other were lining up. The course was formidable, but not enough to really con-

65

cern him. The Ovaro took more rugged jumps during a hard day's ride through the Colorado territory, and in setting it as a twice-around course, they had unwittingly played into his hands. But he'd have to ride a careful, smart race if he was to win.

He took in Jeremy Tallant's horse as the man rode up to the starting line. It was a big gray horse with plenty of power for jumping, but it contained an expression in its eyes that made Fargo smile to himself. This was a horse that would grow unruly when he grew tired and was forced beyond his limits.

Fargo moved the Ovaro to the end of the horses that had lined up ready to go. Gail, astride the dark-sable standardbred, glanced over at him with quiet confidence. She'd positioned herself just off the center of the line, he saw admiringly, a perfect spot, where she could avoid being boxed in and still stay up front. Jeremy Tallant was directly in the center. He plainly intended to use his horse's speed to avoid being jammed, but Fargo figured he'd pay for that later.

Fargo's eyes went to the starter, a dignified gentleman in a black frock coat with embroidered hunting horns on the lapels. From atop a small grandstand, the man raised his silver starter's pistol. Fargo saw Gail half-rise in the saddle as the gun went off, the sound almost drowned out by the cheers of the onlookers.

He let the speed horses race off to take their places out front and saw that Jeremy Tallant had burst forward into the clear without being jammed. He sent the Ovaro forward and fell into the third line of horses that followed the leaders. Gail was behind Jeremy Tallant, and a half-dozen other horses rode close together as they headed out across country. Tallant on the big gray was setting a fast pace, his object to burn out his competition or have them make mistakes to stay with him. His strategy was working, Fargo saw, as two horses went down at the first hogback and a third missed a hedge barrier, all because they forced their mounts.

Fargo let a half-dozen horses pass him in their effort to stay close to the leaders and saw two more go down at a high open-ditch jump. Tom Bonnard was among the horses directly in front of him, and Fargo noted that Jeremy Tallant had opened a good lead over everyone except Gail, who stayed close behind him. Fargo let the Ovaro breeze almost casually, enjoying the powerful ease with which the horse took the high post-and-rail fence.

A big chestnut nearby balked and threw his rider a dozen feet as Fargo sailed over the jump. The Ovaro was running easily as they reached the middle point of the course, and he saw Gail Bonnard look back, her eyes searching the field. She spotted him, and he thought he caught a faint expression of smugness on her face as she turned away. He let the Ovaro extend himself a little more, and the horse quickly made up a dozen seconds as two more mounts went down at a chicken-coop jump.

Tom Bonnard had moved up to become part of the cluster of horses behind the leaders, and Fargo saw the man cast a quick glance back at him. Fargo continued to ride the Ovaro easily behind the lead pack as the other horses began to string out. A young rider on a white Arabian kept pace with him, he noted, and he saw Jeremy Tallant glance back, spot him, and go on. Tallant continued the blistering pace, and Fargo's eyes narrowed as he watched the other horses tiring fast. The big gray didn't have the kind of stamina Tallant expected. Moreover, the horse wasn't the kind to push.

Fargo guided the Ovaro into the circle where another deep open ditch—this one filled with water—came up. Three already tired standardbreds went out on the jump, and Fargo let the Ovaro take it at his own pace. He glanced back and saw the white Arabian staying close as the curve turned into the straightaway that became the starting point. Tallant kept his sizable lead on everyone except Gail as he swept under the banners and went into the second leg of the course.

Tom Bonnard's horse was beginning to strain, Fargo noted, but the men still hung in there. Fargo let the Ovaro out a little further and drew up on Bonnard. He was almost abreast of the man as they headed back into open country and the first stone fence. He saw Gail continue to hang close behind Tallant. She was riding a smart race, he muttered silently, if her horse had the power to outlast Tallant's. Fargo returned his gaze to Tom Bonnard as they reached the stone fence, and he watched Bonnard just clear the barrier. The white Arabian took the jump well, and Fargo saw the hogback coming next. He increased the Ovaro's pace and saw the Arabian come after him, and he let the Ovaro go into the jump full out. The Arabian tried to do the same and went down. Fargo's eyes were on Bonnard as he barely cleared the jump.

A post-and-rail fence came next, and Fargo saw Tom Bonnard take his crop to his horse just before he reached the fence. Fargo saw the horses ears flatten—a sign the animal knew he was unable to properly collect himself for the jump. He saw the horse half-turn, and throw his forelegs out stiffly. Tom Bonnard flew from the saddle, crashed into the fence, and sprawled beneath it. As the Ovaro cleared the jump, Fargo saw bystanders running to aid Tom Bonnard's sprawled figure.

Fargo focused on Jeremy Tallant and Gail just in front of him, allowing the Ovaro to go out further. He leaned down and listened. He heard the horse breathing easily, his hooves pounding the ground in a long, unlabored stride. There were only three horses between him and the two leaders—all of them losing strength fast. The Ovaro steadily closed in on them. A stone fence with an added rail appeared, and the three horses went down, one swerving to avoid the jump altogether. Fargo caught Tallant's quick glance back at him and saw the frown on the man's face. Gail knew he was there too, he smiled grimly. She didn't waste concentration to look back but used the time to creep closer to Tallant. Fargo touched the Ovaro on the rump. At the light slap of his hand, the horse surged forward, coming up on Gail.

This time she did glance back, and he saw the frown on her face. She took the crop to the dark sable and the horse closed in on Jeremy Tallant, whose horse was now breathing hard. The Ovaro was running smoothly, and Fargo drew closer to Gail as she flung him another glance.

He pulled the Ovaro to the right to give himself plenty of room as a high-hedge jump came into sight. Tallant looked back, alarm in his face now, and Fargo saw him having trouble holding the big gray's head up. The horse managed the hedge jump, and Fargo took it at the same moment Gail sent her mount over. The last jump lay just ahead, and Fargo saw Tallant's big gray's eyes dilating. Exactly as he'd expected, the gray wasn't a horse that could be pushed beyond his own limit. Fargo heard Jeremy Tallant's curses as the gray fought bit and rider.

Fargo glanced at Gail as he began to pull ahead of

her, the Ovaro drawing on the endurance and power gathered in the hard-riding mountains and the vast plains of his western homeland.

The dark sable was a half-length behind, and Fargo smiled. He had put Gail away, he was confident, and had only to overtake Tallant, who was losing ground fast as he fought the gray. Fargo pulled the Ovaro to the right so he could take the last jump freely. He rose in the saddle as the horse began to collect himself for the open ditch and the high hedge. But suddenly Tallant's big gray tore away from his control, and Fargo saw the horse cut directly in front of him and take the jump at a sideways angle. The Ovaro's front feet had already left the ground, and Fargo cursed as he watched the gray land on the other side of the barrier directly in front of him. Utterly helpless, Fargo clung to his mount as the Ovaro slammed into the gray's rump. Tallant's horse skidded to the side and the Ovaro stumbled forward. Fargo gave the horse his head, then leaned back to help the horse balance himself, and the Ovaro managed to avoid going down.

But the horse's rhythmn as well as his speed had been broken, and Fargo pulled on him to try to bring him back into control. Tallant's gray fought its rider's efforts to bring him around. But Gail had sailed over the jump cleanly, and Fargo saw her racing to the curve that went into the straightaway of the finish line.

"Goddammit," he yelled, and leaned low over the Ovaro's neck. He slammed the horse hard on the rump and felt the animal respond instantly, surging forward with all the power in his magnificently conditioned, muscled body.

But Gail was into the straightaway, somehow getting a last thrust out of her laboring, winded mount. "Shit," Fargo flung into the wind as he flattened himself down over the Ovaro's jet-black neck. He had ridden his race perfectly, gauged each horse absolutely on target, only to lose because Jeremy Tallant's gray had gone out of control. He swore again and saw that he was gaining on Gail Bonnard as the finish line grew perilously close. He wondered what was keeping her horse going. Even as the thought flew through his mind, he saw her mount stumble, falter, break stride.

But Gail Bonnard was an expert rider. He swore silently as she collected the horse and avoided breaking stride more than he had. The Ovaro was now abreast of her, its powerful, driving strides devouring the ground. The finish line was but a dozen yards away, and the Ovaro, sensing it, extended himself further. Fargo saw Gail dropping back. He was almost four lengths ahead of her as he swept past the finish marker.

Easing the Ovaro back, he let the horse slow itself down at its own pace. He heard the cheers and applause of the crowd as he made a wide circle with the Ovaro and rode back to the finish line at a slow trot.

Gail had dismounted, he saw, and someone had come to take her horse to walk it down. There was grudging admiration in her eyes as he dismounted. "Congratulations," she said, and offered a slow smile. "An impressive ride. I underestimated both you and your horse."

"It's been done before," he said mildly.

Perspiration made her face shine and wisps of hair fell out from beneath her riding cap, and it all made her look less contained but no less lovely.

"You won. Pick your day," Gail said.

"Tomorrow," he said, and saw her brows arch.

"So quickly? Should I feel flattered?"

"Feel lucky." Fargo smiled.

The gray eyes narrowed a fraction. "I see you don't believe in modesty," she said.

"Sometimes. Mostly modesty's for those who need it," he said. "I'll come by midmorning."

"I'll be ready," she said, and he felt her eyes studying him with cool amusement as he moved the Ovaro on. He saw Jeremy Tallant leading the big gray through the crowd, the man's face sullen with anger. Fargo turned the Ovaro away from the thickest concentration of people and skirted the edge of the crowd to spot Tom Bonnard. The man was on foot, his head bandaged, a bruise over one eye, and his hunting coat ripped at the shoulder. He was headed for where Gail had taken her mount, and he paused to talk with some onlookers. Fargo had started to turn the horse away from the large tent when he heard his name called out, and he turned to see Joe Alcott, notepad in hand.

"I was about to come looking for you," Fargo said. "Didn't figure you'd be here."

"This is a big social event around here. I had to cover it for the paper," Alcott said. "But I certainly didn't expect you'd be here. And racing, to boot."

Fargo smiled broadly. "My horse was challenged last night," he said. "Can you leave now?"

"I can. I'll get my horse," Joe said.

Fargo waited till he returned on a piebald mare. He rode alongside Alcott in silence until they had left the area of the meet and the crowds. "Found that house I told you about," he said finally, and Joe Alcott's brows lifted in surprise.

"No kidding? Where?" Joe asked.

"It's called Dark Willows," Fargo said.

72

Joe Alcott reined to a halt and stared at him in astonishment. "That's the Bonnard place."

"Bull's-eye," Fargo grunted.

"It can't be. Your eyes must have played tricks on you in that storm. You're mistaken. You saw a house that looked like the Bonnards'," Alcott said.

"No tricks, no mistake. That's the house," Fargo replied.

"I've never heard of any little blonde and giant hulk living at the Bonnards'. It just can't be. You've got to be wrong," Joe insisted.

"That's the house," Fargo repeated doggedly.

"I don't believe it. I can't understand it," Joe said.

"I aim to find out more," Fargo growled.

Joe Alcott peered at him for a long moment as they rode on. "I understand that you want your revenge, but you've come here to find something else, Fargo," the man reminded.

"I know that. I don't plan to let one interfere with the other. That's the other reason I was coming to find you. There are two roads and a riverbank I want patrolled every night, for a few nights at least. That means we need another man, somebody reliable," he said.

"Bill Howes," Joe Alcott said at once. "Bill's no spring chicken anymore, but he's a good man and a niece of his disappeared some six months back. We can stop at his place now if you want."

"Let's go," Fargo said, and Alcott turned from the road to cut across the bright-green orchard grass. At the far side of a low hill they drew up to a neat house in a long grove of pecan trees. A small, wiry-built man with a short gray beard emerged from beneath a row of trees with a wicker basket full of pecans. Alcott made the introductions and explained how Ned Simmons had sent for Fargo.

"Whatever you need, just ask," Bill Howes said grimly. "But the sheriff's patrols came up empty, you know. He finally called them off. What makes you think you'll do better?" he asked the big man.

"Timing, luck, maybe. Or maybe the sheriff had riders too easy to spot," Fargo said. "I want one man per road. I want you to ride up and down and watch. If you see something, anything that bothers you, hang back and watch, trail if you can. Mostly, you come get me. The roads and the riverbank aren't far apart."

"I understand," Bill Howes said. "I'll get my horse."

Fargo nodded, sat back, and waited until the man reappeared on a small but chunky bay gelding. They set out across the gentle hills as dusk slid over the land, and when they reached the first road, Fargo said, "You take this one, Joe. You take the riverbank, Bill. I'll patrol the road in between. That way either of you can come get me quickly. Fire three fast shots if there's real trouble."

Both men nodded, and Joe Alcott started to turn his horse down the road.

"We meet back here when the moon has headed halfway down to tomorrow," Fargo called out, then moved on as dark descended like a silent curtain.

Bill Howes hurried on toward the riverbank and Fargo toward the center road. A half-moon rose in the sky, and once again the Trailsman noted how low the brush cover was along the roadside. There were a few places where hickory and black willow clustered, but mostly there was just low brush. A man would have to practically lie down in the brush not to be seen. He frowned at that thought as he rode at a slow trot. He went on for about two miles, retraced steps, and went up the road in the other direction. He added another mile and turned back again. By the time the half-moon had begun to slide toward the dawn horizon, he had patrolled more than a dozen miles. And seen or heard nothing, he grunted to himself.

Fargo halted as he saw Joe and Bill Howes appear. "Nothing," both men muttered.

"Same thing tomorrow night," Fargo said as he turned the Ovaro and headed across the grass. "It'd sure help if we knew there was a stage or a carriage due with some young ladies aboard."

"I'll ask around tomorrow," Joe Alcott said. "Maybe somebody will know something. Besides, folks are used to my nosing around with questions."

"Good," Fargo said as he turned to veer off alone. "Same place tomorrow night." He sent the horse into a canter, found a big black locust, and bedded down under it. He went to sleep, still wondering how a stage could be attacked by surprise from so little roadside cover. Sleep smothered idling conjecture, and he woke only when the warm sun slid its way under the branches of the locust. He found a small stream and washed, breakfasting on peaches and pecans he came across as he walked the pinto slowly along the stream. He swung onto the horse, finally, and headed for the Bonnard place.

As he drew up before the tall, white columns and the tall arched windows, the surge of anger spiraled through him at once. He had nearly met his death in this aristocratic mansion, and he damn sure was going to find out why. He guided the Ovaro to one side of the house, taking in the spotless white corral fences in back, the well-tended grounds and barns. A horse and rider emerged from the main barn, and he saw Gail Bonnard come toward him on a tan gelding. She wore a light-gray blouse that matched her eyes and tan jodhpurs that revealed a nice, round rear that balanced the fullness of her breasts. Her smile was contained, and her gray eyes danced with their own private amusement.

"You're prompt, but I expected that," she said.

"How's your brother?" Fargo asked, and she nodded past him.

"Ask him yourself," she said, and he turned to see Tom Bonnard stepping out of the house. He wore the bandage on his head and carried a bruise over one eye, but his step was crisp.

"Bad fall, that was," Fargo commented.

"Yes, I should've known my horse was done in. You rode a very smart race," the man said, his face unsmiling.

"And Tallant rode a stupid one," Fargo said. "Led you all along with him, too."

"I'd have taken him by the finish line," Gail protested.

"Yes, probably," Fargo agreed.

"Enjoy your day," Tom Bonnard said, and Fargo caught the quick, sharp glance he flicked at his sister.

Gail Bonnard brought her mount up alongside the Ovaro, and Fargo rode beside her as she set out across country. "Anything special in mind?" she asked.

"Thought I'd let you show me the countryside," Fargo said.

Her glance was one of appraising amusement. "Didn't take you for the sight-seeing type," she remarked.

"Never go by looks," he said, and her smile told him she didn't accept the answer. But she took him across the mostly flat countryside, pointing out the stately mansions and the potato, sugarcane, pecan, and cotton plantations. He saw lots of thick, rich bluegrass and shallow streams that crisscrossed the countryside almost as though they were a network of irrigation avenues. Only when he pointed to a line of willows not far from her own home did she balk.

"How about back there, the bayou country, I'm told," he said.

"No, I never go near it," Gail Bonnard said. "I can't stand it. It gives me the creeps." A little shiver ran through her, and she turned her horse around. "You'll have to get someone else to take you in there," she said firmly.

He followed her as she rode over a long field of partridge peas and turned in under a cluster of black walnut where the fragrant leaves offered cool shelter from the scorchingly hot afternoon sun. She swung lightly from her horse, taking a small leather pouch with her, folded herself on the grass, and leaned back against one of the tree trunks.

He liked the way she moved. She had a grace to her and an ease of movement that gave her an air of fluidity even sitting still. Her gray eyes continued to regard him with quiet amusement as he dismounted and sat down beside her. She reached into the leather pouch, drew out two silver goblets and a small hide-covered jug.

"Southern hospitality," Gail Bonnard said as she poured from the jug and handed him one of the goblets.

He sipped from the goblet and tasted the rich, smooth, slightly sweet liquid, then tossed Gail a quizzical glance.

"A special blend we make. It's a bourbon-based liqueur," she said.

"Damn nice," he said as he took another pull on the goblet. Gail leaned back against a tree trunk, and the gray blouse rested atop the slightly concave line of her breasts. "Damn nice," he repeated, and she allowed a slow smile. He leaned onto one elbow near

77

her. "I'm told the Bonnards own most of Thurmond county and control what they don't own," he said.

"Now, wherever did you hear that?" she returned lightly.

"I was talking to Joe Alcott," Fargo said.

"Ah, our local newspaperman," Gail said. "Joe tends to exaggerate. Daddy did gather a lot of land and good working properties, God rest his soul."

"You and your brother carrying on?" Fargo asked.

"Of course," Gail said. "Nothing wrong in that."

"Not a thing," Fargo agreed.

Her gray eyes studied him as she spoke. "I watched you while we rode. You noticed every special mark, every tree that was different, every rock formation, every twisted stream that came up," she said.

"Habit," he said, and her brows lifted. "Some folks call me the Trailsman," he explained.

"I see," Gail murmured. "What's brought you here?"

"The disappearances of all those young women," he answered. "I expect you know about that. I understand it's common knowledge."

"Yes, it's a major concern of everyone. I hardly go out at night any longer because of all that's happened," she said. "But it seems impossible to stop."

"If there's a trail, it can be stopped," Fargo said.

"Who called you in on this?" Gail asked.

"An old friend, Ned Simmons. His daughter, Cynthia, disappeared. He put me in touch with Joe Alcott," Fargo told her. He drained the goblet and handed it to her.

"Another drink?" she asked.

"No, that'll do fine for now," he answered, and watched as she sat up straighter, pulled the leather pouch to her, and started to return the jug and goblets to it. He kept his voice casual as he slid the question at her. "Now you tell me something, honey. Who was the pretty blonde and the giant in your cellar a half-dozen days ago?" he asked. He watched Gail Bonnard stiffen at the question, and one of the goblets drop from her hand.

"Clumsy," she muttered as she leaned forward, picked up the goblet, pushed it into the pouch, and turned a quizzical frown at him. "Whatever are you talking about?" Gail Bonnard asked with almost sweet curiosity, and he credited her with a quick recovery.

"The little blonde, hair sort of uncombed, but a very pretty face and blue-fire eyes," Fargo said.

"I don't know anyone who looks like that," Gail Bonnard said.

"Big, bald-headed monster with her. They were in your cellar," Fargo repeated calmly.

"Not in Dark Willows. You've made some sort of mistake, I'm afraid, Fargo," Gail said.

"No mistake," Fargo grunted firmly.

"Of course there is. Just what is this all about, anyway?" Gail queried.

"It's about finding your house in a blinding storm and damn near getting killed for it," Fargo said, and quickly told her the details. She listened, and he watched as her face grew paler with his every word. When he finished, the shock in her face was real, he was certain.

"Good God, what a terrible story. But it didn't happen at Dark Willows. You're mistaken about that. It was some other house," Gail insisted.

"Your house," Fargo muttered adamantly.

"No, impossible. It couldn't be. It had to be somewhere else," she returned. She paused, her eyes narrowing. "Is that why you were sneaking about in the cellar?"

"Yes," he admitted, and held back mentioning the cleaned away bloodstained area. He'd find out what she was hiding first, he decided.

"Well, it wasn't Dark Willows," Gail repeated, trying not to sound defensive. "You really have made a mistake there. It had to be some other one of the big houses. You can believe me, Fargo."

He shrugged and smiled. "I never argue with a lady," he said.

"That's not saying you believe me." Gail frowned.

"No, it isn't," he agreed affably. "You'll have to convince me," he said, and his hand closed around the back of her neck and drew her to him. He found her lips with his, soft and warm as he kissed her slowly, firmly. She allowed no real response but didn't pull away, either. He pressed his lips harder and opened her mouth. He felt the tip of her tongue as her lips tightened, opened, responded, and then she was pushing both hands against his chest. He let her go. Two tiny dots of color had come to her cheeks, he saw.

"You can convince better than that," he chided.

"I might try if it'd work," she said.

"It might work if you try." He laughed.

Her gray eyes studied his face. "No, not with you it wouldn't," she decided.

His hand closed around the back of her neck again, smooth skin, tiny wisps of hair coming in between his fingers. "All right, no convincing, just fun," he said, and pressed his mouth to hers. He felt her lips come open and soften for him, and he pulled her closer. Her breasts pushed against his chest, flattening into soft warmth before she pushed away.

"No, I must get back," Gail Bonnard murmured, but he caught the gray fire of desire in her eyes before she fought it down. "I have to play hostess for Tom tonight. He's running for senator from Thurmond county and some influential people are coming to dinner."

Fargo half-shrugged, stepped back, and watched her climb onto the tan gelding, her very round rear slipping perfectly onto the saddle. He mounted the Ovaro and rode off beside her. She occupied the ride back with mostly meaningless chatter, and he saw the tiny lines of tension cling to the corners of her lovely mouth. He slid from the saddle when they halted before the big house as the day began to turn to night.

"I just might come by again," Fargo said.

"I just might look forward to it," Gail said, and stood very close to him as she let her fingers trace a little line down the front of his shirt with studied idleness. "I do want you to believe me about that girl and Dark Willows," she murmured.

"I'll think about it," he said, and she stepped back, a hint of satisfaction touching her eyes.

"Good night, Fargo," she said, and hurried into the house as night descended.

Fargo walked the Ovaro away, continued on until he reached a big weeping willow, and pulled the horse into its black shadows. He crouched down, his eyes on the house. He saw the main room brightly lighted through the tall, arched windows. He left the Ovaro, went into a long, loping crouch, and crossed the open space to the house. Creeping to the nearest of the arched windows, he peered in to see Gail and her brother in the foyer, Tom Bonnard in evening dress. Tense anger shrouded his face, and he gesticulated sharply as he and Gail exchanged words.

Fargo made a silent wager she'd told him about the blonde. He continued to watch and noted that Gail remained the calmer of the two as Tom Bonnard bit out words, his lips a tight line.

Fargo dropped down as he heard the sound of a horse and carriage drawing near. He edged his way from the window, darted through the darkness, and dropped to one knee beside a hedge as he saw a coachman and a dark-red full clarence draw up to the front of the house. Two men and a woman, all in evening capes, emerged from the clarence and went into the house as the butler opened the tall front door. Fargo backed from the hedge, stayed in a crouch until he reached the Ovaro beneath the willow, and walked the horse away. He swung into the saddle when he'd gone another dozen yards from the big house and rode into the darkness as he let the day wind back through his thoughts.

Somehow, someway, Gail Bonnard knew about the little blonde. Her reaction had proven that much despite her quick recovery and all her denials. His description of the girl had shaken her, and it was plain that she was hiding something. Both she and Tom Bonnard had been visibly upset. Why, if they didn't know the little blonde? he pondered. What strange connection could there be between her and the contained, assured Gail Bonnard and her powerful heritage? There sure didn't seem any way to fit it together, Fargo mused. But Gail's vehement denials had a hollow ring to them. He had come onto something damn strange, and he'd see it through. It was personal now. He didn't like damn near being killed and left for dead. He didn't like being lied to about it much better. Gail Bonnard, for all her wealth and assured beauty, would find out that he could play her game and beat her at it. He'd damn well find out what was behind those gray eyes.

He slowed as he saw the two figures waiting at the

road. "Was starting to worry about you," Joe Alcott said.

"Sorry," Fargo apologized. "Got hung up visiting with Gail Bonnard. Tell you more later. Let's patrol." He led the way to the second road, Bill Howes at his heels, watched the straight, graying figure ride on toward the riverbank, and turned the Ovaro up the road. He used the same method he had the night before, riding slowly up and down the road as his eyes searched the low brush and the land just beyond. Once again, as the long night wore on, he saw nothing, heard nothing, and yet, as the moon hung high in the blue velvet sky, he felt an uneasiness curl in the pit of his stomach.

Something stalked the darkness, something he failed to see, but it was there, he was sure. He rode slowly, peering back at the land just behind the brush that bordered the road on both sides. He saw nothing and swore softly as he patrolled back and forth, but the uneasiness stayed with him. When the moon finally slid down the far reaches of the sky, he turned the Ovaro back to meet Alcott and Howes. His eyes hurt from straining through the dark, and he wondered if his uneasiness had merely been the result of tension and tiredness.

He discarded the thought. His instincts were invariably right. Something strange had been near. He slowed as Bill Howes rode up and then Joe Alcott. They had seen only silent darkness also, and rode tiredly across the fields with him. When Bill Howes turned off, Alcott rode on another quarter mile.

"You'd something to tell me about Gail Bonnard," Alcott reminded him.

"I told her about the girl in the house. She insisted I had the wrong house," Fargo said. "But she was lying. She knows something. Tom Bonnard too."

Joe Alcott listened with a growing frown as Fargo told him exactly how Gail had reacted. When he'd finished, the man pushed his hat back and screwed his face up in distaste.

"Sure seems funny, I'll say that much," Joe Alcott muttered. "But there's got to be some logical explanation. Gail and Tom Bonnard and a murderous little blonde? Hell, it doesn't fit. I've been to Dark Willows a good number of times on one story or another— usually some big party they were holding—and I never saw anyone that fits your description of the girl."

"I aim to find out the truth of it," Fargo growled as Alcott halted at the spot where he turned west to St. Lucifer.

"See you tomorrow night." Alcott waved as he rode on, and Fargo cantered on to bed down under the same big black locust where he'd slept the night before. He stretched out, refusing to let whirling questions steal even a precious second of sleep, and shut out the world.

He slept heavily until morning woke him, and he sat up, his plans for the day already formed in his mind. Gail Bonnard was at the center of them. Spending time with her was the first step. He wanted to give her the chance to slip up, make a mistake, or simply reveal more than she intended. He thought about the quietly amused gray eyes, the full, lovely breasts. At the very least, he'd enjoy pursuing the truth, he grunted as he hurried to the stream, washed, and breakfasted on wild plums and the sweet acorns of a water oak. When he'd finished, he pointed the pinto toward the Bonnard house. He'd come halfway there when, in surprise, he saw the dark-sable standardbred moving across the flat field.

He rode out from the shade of a line of chestnuts

and waited for Gail Bonnard to see him. When she did, she turned the horse toward him at once.

"Morning ride?" he asked as she reached him. She had on an off-white, silk blouse that clung to the full breasts with shiny provocativeness, and for the first time he caught the outline of tiny points under the material.

"I came looking for you," Gail said. "I imagined you'd bed down not too far away."

"Looking for me? I like that." Fargo smiled.

"Don't run off with the bit, Fargo," she said crisply. "I've the answer to what happened to you."

Fargo's brows lifted. "Oh?" he murmured.

"You're still convinced the house was Dark Willows, I take it," she said, and he nodded. "Well, you may be right," she continued, and his brows rose further. "I spoke to Tom about what you'd said, and he reminded me of something. The house was empty a week ago."

"Empty?" Fargo frowned.

"Exactly. You see, Tom and I divide our time between here and New Orleans. We were in New Orleans at the time of the storm. And the house was empty."

"No servants there, nobody at all?" Fargo asked.

"Nobody," Gail repeated firmly. "We let the servants go off to their friends or relatives. The house was closed down completely. Obviously, this pair broke in."

"You find any signs of a break-in?" Fargo asked.

Gail paused for a half-moment. "No, but you got in through the storm-cellar door," she answered. "I imagine they did the same. They were there for days, perhaps, when you arrived, and they decided they couldn't let you get away to tell anyone."

Fargo's lips pursed in thought as he turned her

words in his mind. He finally offered a slow, rueful smile. "Sure seems to explain what happened," he said.

"Yes, it does. Common thieves or perhaps runaways broke into the house, and you happened onto them," Gail said with satisfied finality in her voice.

"Tom thought of this, did he?" Fargo asked pleasantly.

"Yes, I'd simply forgotten that we were away then," Gail said. "It really quite clears up all the mystery, doesn't it?"

"Seems to." Fargo smiled.

"Now you can concentrate on what really brought you down here, those strange disappearances," Gail said. "Any leads so far?"

"Not yet," Fargo said. "I was going to stop at a little lake I saw just beyond the next low rise. How about keeping me company?"

Gail paused in thought, her gray eyes fixed on him. "I shouldn't. Jeremy usually comes calling Tuesdays. He expects me at home."

"I got here first this Tuesday. Besides, Tallant's not your kind of drink," Fargo said.

"Meaning what?" Gail frowned, but her eyes danced.

"Why turn down a mint julep for a lemonade?" Fargo answered.

She laughed softly. "Why," she echoed, "especially now that you understand about the girl in the house."

"Especially," he repeated, and put the Ovaro into a slow trot.

She swung her horse alongside him. "I really don't know why I'm doing this." She frowned.

"Because you can have lemonade anytime," Fargo tossed back. He quickened the horse's canter until he pulled up before the small lake with a half-circle of willows at one end. The Louisiana sun had grown hot quickly, and he tethered the horse under the trees. Gail did the same and slid from the saddle. When she turned, he had his shirt off. He stripped off gun belt and boots as Gail's eyes held on him, traveled across the width of his shoulders, the highly developed pectorals, the smooth power of his body. He saw the tip of her tongue move across her lips. He decided not to strip trousers off. She wasn't the kind to throw too much at too quickly. He turned, slipped into the water, and found it warm but refreshing.

He swam, dived, came up, turned in the water playfully, moved to the edge, and rose half out. The sun glistened on the beauty and power of his deltoids, turning his chest into shining magnificence. His eyes fastened on Gail Bonnard and saw the little pinpoints of darkness in the depths of her pupils. "Going to join me?" he challenged.

"I don't have a bathing suit," she murmured.

"Neither do I," he said, and saw the tiny smile come to her full red lips. Gail Bonnard liked challenges, excitement. He already knew that much about her. Refusing a dare would come hard to her, and he pushed again. "You challenged me to a race," he said.

"And now you're challenging me," she returned.

"I took you up on it," he reminded her.

Her eyes narrowed. "So you did."

He watched her fingers undo the top button of the silk blouse. She moved her hand down slowly, undoing each button until the blouse hung open. She shrugged it from her shoulders, revealing the chemise she wore underneath. She pulled the bottom part of it up out of the waistband of the jodhpurs and flung it over her head to stand bare-breasted before him. His eyes fastened on the twin, creamy-white mounds, fuller than they'd seemed under the blouses she had worn. Her nipples were small and very pink, on equally pink little areolae, breasts that were both womanly and yet somehow virginally creamy. As he watched, she stepped out of the jodhpurs and riding boots. She wore long, pink bloomers with lace edges, the material heavy enough to cover her with complete modesty from waist to knees. She flashed a smile at him as she stepped into the lake.

"I'm joining you for a swim, nothing else," Gail said. She slid into the water and turned on her back, her breasts rising up with magnificent provocativeness. She turned, dived, came up, and flashed him another smile. She had taken his challenge and turned it back on him, he realized with admiration. She had style as well as class.

He swam alongside her, watched as she lazily played in the water and deliberately let her cream-white breasts surface, glistening wet and beautiful, then disappear underneath again. She was teasing him, returning what he had done to her. She was doing a damn good job of it, he realized, and he dived deep into the lake where the water remained cool and untouched by the sun. He surfaced finally to see her climb out of the water and fold herself onto the grass in the sun as little droplets of water shimmered on the creamy breasts and trickled down between their full loveliness.

The long bloomers, even soaking wet, kept the rest of her concealed in complete modesty, but he saw the line of long, curving thighs as she crossed her legs. Damn her, he murmured silently, and climbed out of the water to stand before her. He flicked buttons open, stepped out of his wet trousers, aware that his maleness had responded to her tantalizing beauty and filled his underwear. He watched her eyes linger on his crotch as her lips parted, and he heard the soft intake of her breath. But she remained motionless even as her face took on a faint flush and her eyes stayed fastened on him.

He dropped to his knees, reached out, and gently drew one finger across her shoulder, tracing a path down the wetness of her skin, over her collarbone and down across one soft breast. She didn't move, but he saw her eyes half-close and her lips drew breath in with a long gasp. His finger moved lightly down farther. He traced a line on the top of her full breast, drawing near the very pink nipple.

Suddenly she flung herself sideways, rolled, came up on one knee a half-dozen feet from him, and her gray eyes speared him with turbulent anger.

"No," she gasped out. "This time I win."

"Do you?" he slid back.

"Yes," Gail Bonnard said, the word hissed with determined firmness. More than enough truth in it, he swore inwardly as he felt the desire surging through his loins, his thick, throbbing maleness straining against his underclothes. He searched her face, and saw the turbulence of her eyes still held, although her breath continued to draw in with sharp little gasps.

"Guess again, honey," he said as he swore silently and flung himself onto his back, forcing the urges of the flesh into control. He lay very still as his raging emotions subsided, and he saw Gail sink down on the grass, keeping her distance. The hot sun finally dried him, inside as well as outside, and the afternoon sky began to lengthen. He half-dozed in the restful quiet and snapped his eyes open when he heard Gail stir. He pushed himself onto one elbow and watched her walk to where she had left her

89

clothes. She moved straight-backed, the cream breasts held high, swinging softly in unison as she started to pull on clothes. He waited till she buttoned the blouse before he rose and dressed, and when she faced him, he saw that the gray smokiness still smoldered in her eyes.

"Would you settle for a dead heat?" she said.

He shrugged. "Good enough, especially the heat part." He grinned. Her face softened, and he stepped forward and pulled her into his arms. Her lips were open as he pressed his mouth on them, and he felt her tongue slide across his teeth, pull back, dart forward and retreat at once. Her breasts were smoothly soft against him under the silk blouse. She pulled away finally, the gray eyes peering hard at him.

"Down payment on next time," Fargo said.

"What makes you think there'll be a next time?" she questioned with arched brows.

"What makes you think there won't?" He laughed, turned from her, and swung onto the Ovaro. He waited as she mounted the dark sable and swung in beside her.

"Seeing me home? Unexpected gallantry," she said, an edge of sarcasm to her tone.

"Practicing at being a southern gentleman." Fargo laughed.

"More like playacting," Gail sniffed.

"Some folks playact at one thing, some at another," he remarked.

She did not pursue the statement as they rode across the fields in the late-afternoon shadows.

Tom Bonnard came from the house as they rode to a halt, and Gail dismounted quickly. Fargo followed with slow casualness. "Expected you back long ago," the man said to his sister. "Jeremy waited most of the day before he left. He wasn't happy."

"I expect not," Gail said. "I decided to enjoy the day with Fargo. He understands about the girl in the house, now," she said to her brother, and Fargo caught the pointedness of her tone.

"Well, I'm glad we cleared that up," Tom Bonnard said to Fargo with a measured smile.

"I didn't say that," Fargo slid out casually, and saw Gail's thin brows knit at once.

"You said it explained things." She frowned at him.

"Correction, honey. I said it seemed that way. I didn't say it did," Fargo answered blandly.

"But it does," Gail said sharply.

"Afraid not." Fargo smiled.

"Of course it does," Tom Bonnard cut in angrily.

Fargo fastened Tom Bonnard with a calm stare. "You clean it up?" be asked.

"Clean what up?" Bonnard frowned.

"Figured not." Fargo laughed.

"What are you talking about?" Bonnard almost shouted.

"I bashed the hulk's head in, and he spilled blood all over the middle of your cellar floor. I saw it was cleaned up. You just admitted you didn't do it, and the servants weren't in the house. People that break into a house don't trouble themselves to clean up afterward. They also steal, and nothing was stolen. I didn't come onto a pair of thieves who'd broken into your house," Fargo concluded.

"What are you saying, Fargo?" Tom Bonnard roared.

"You tell me," Fargo snapped.

"I've nothing to tell you. You were told what we thought happened. Now, I'm thinking you've made the whole story up just to get Gail's attentions," Bonnard shouted.

"Good try, but no cigar." Fargo laughed as Bonnard spun, and stormed to the big house. Fargo walked to the Ovaro and halted as Gail came up to him.

"Bastard," she hissed. "You let me think you believed me."

"You let yourself think it," he told her.

"Nothing happened to you at Dark Willows, Fargo. Forget it, dammit, just forget it," she said, then whirled and ran into the house.

He watched her slam the stately door behind her. He almost felt sorry for her, but not enough to back off. Maybe she knew the truth, or maybe she was trapped into something that involved her brother. Either way, he'd still find out, and he still had a score to settle.

Fargo climbed onto the pinto and rode until he found a big willow. He pulled the horse under the trailing fronds. Focusing his gaze back at the big house, he grunted when he saw Tom Bonnard emerge, hurry into the stables, and race out on a black Arab. The man raced across the flat field, and Fargo cursed softly. Daylight still clung to the land and Bonnard would easily see him if he tried to follow across the open fields. He watched Tom Bonnard ride out of sight over a low rise, waited a few minutes longer before moving out from under the tree.

Day was fading fast, but he picked up the fresh hoofprints in the thick grass easily enough. He hung back to be sure he wouldn't be seen. He had crossed half the field and was heading toward the top of a low rise when he saw the horse coming toward him out of the dusk. He recognized the big gray hunter at once and reined to a halt as Jeremy Tallant came up to him. The man was dressed in gentleman's riding clothes, a gray jacket and gray britches, a silk cravat around his neck.

"I thought you'd be somewhere near Gail's place," Jeremy Tallant glowered. "I've been waiting for you."

"I'm busy. I can't play games with you now," Fargo growled.

"You're not too busy to hear what I have to say. You're to stay away from Gail Bonnard, Fargo," Tallant ordered.

"Isn't that her business?" Fargo returned.

"Gail is too well-bred to handle your type," the man snapped.

"What type is that?" Fargo asked mildly.

"Crude, ungentlemanly, compelling, with an animal forcefulness. Gail is too much the lady to deal with you properly. She's probably somewhat frightened by you," Tallant said.

"Hell she is." Fargo laughed.

"I'm not interested in what you think. You're to stop forcing your attentions on her. Stay away from her, do you hear me?" Tallant said with autocratic sharpness.

"Sorry, we've some unfinished business. You can have her when I'm through with her," Fargo said. "Now get the hell out of my way."

"By God, you're an insulting wretch," Tallant roared as Fargo started to steer the Ovaro around him. Fargo heard the sharp click of a pistol hammer drawn back as Tallant shouted at him. "Stop or I'll put a bullet through your shameless hide," the man ordered.

Fargo halted, turned in the saddle, and saw Jeremy Tallant had a heavy-barreled French-made dueling pistol in his hand.

"Get off that horse. I'm going to teach you a lesson," the man ordered

Fargo cursed under his breath. The heavy pistol was aimed dead at his gut, and even a rotten marksman couldn't miss at that range. He slid from th Ovaro, knowing that he could draw and fire before Jeremy Tallant even pulled the trigger. But he didn't want any killing done—not yet, anyway—and not a pathetic fool such as Jeremy Tallant.

"Now what?" Fargo said as he faced the man.

"Drop your gun belt," Tallant said. Fargo unbuckled his belt and let it fall to the ground before dismounting. "Over here," the man ordered, and Fargo stepped away from the gun belt and saw Jeremy Tallant drop his pistol on the ground. "Now I'm going to teach you a lesson in proper behavior," Tallant said.

"You really are a damn fool, Tallant," Fargo said as he cast a glance at the fast-fading light. "Hurry up about it, will you?" he said.

"I'll take that peasant cockiness out of you," Jeremy Tallant spit out, and he stepped forward and let two jabs fly. One caught Fargo a grazing blow along the temple, but he ducked away from two more the man threw at him. Tallant was fast, he saw, but he fought out of an upright stance in proper boxing-ring behavior. He came forward with two more quick jabs that Fargo blocked easily, then threw a short, straight right that missed by inches.

Fargo came toward him with the same upright stance. Tallant moved forward and threw a left hook with all his strength. Fargo's upright stance vanished as he ducked, weaved, brought a ripping uppercut up under Tallant's left. It caught the man flush under his chin, and he went backward. Dropping to one knee, Tallant pulled himself up. He came forward again, and Fargo threw a twisting left that landed on the side of Tallant's jaw, followed by a whistling right, and the man went down.

Tallant quivered and somehow pushed himself to his feet, only to take a sharp left hook that spun him completely around before it dumped him on the ground. He lay still, and Fargo walked over to him, lifted his head up by the hair, and shook him.

Jeremy Tallant's eyes opened.

"You don't fight any better than you race," Fargo said, and let the man's head drop. He returned to the Ovaro, strapped on his gun belt as the night swept across the field. Trailing Tom Bonnard was impossible now, and by the time the moon came up, the thick, fresh grass would have sprung back in place. He swore as he swung onto the Ovaro and started to ride away.

"Fargo, I'm not through with you. Keep away . . . from Gail," he heard Jeremy Tallant call out in pain.

"When I'm finished," Fargo flung back without turning, and sent the pinto into a canter. He slowed when he crested the rise, and his eyes swept the long, flat fields. Nothing but a few clusters of black locust met his gaze, and he rode forward. The moon moved up higher in the sky. It was near time to take up patrolling again, and he put aside one set of unexplained questions for another.

5

The night had brought no more clues than the others had. Once again he'd seen nothing, heard nothing, and Joe Alcott and Bill Howes reported back the same at the night's close. But again, Fargo had felt something, sensed something, yet found himself wondering if tension and expectation were not leading instinct astray.

"Same time, same place tomorrow night?" Bill Howes asked as he started to turn off, and Fargo nodded as he rode on with Joe Alcott.

"I'm more sure than ever now," Fargo said, and the newspaperman returned a quizzical stare. "The Bonnards and the little blonde that tried to kill me—there's some connection." He told what had taken place that day, and when he finished, Joe Alcott reined up with his face wreathed in consternation.

"It makes no damn sense, Fargo," Alcott said. "Why would a gal like that be in their cellar, and why would they be covering it up. I've known Gail and Tom since they were children. They're Bonnards, like their pa, headstrong, ambitious, high-handed, autocratic. They like power, position, wealth. They use what they have to get what they want, especially

Tom. He wants to outdo his pa, and that takes a lot of ambition. But being involved with an attempted murderess, hell, there's no rhyme or reason for that."

"You think I'm reading what I've seen the wrong way," Fargo asked.

"Could be, Fargo," the man said.

"How?" Fargo questioned.

"Well, now, you say Gail was so upset she dropped the goblet. Maybe she really did have it slip out of her hand just at that moment, and you're tying them together. Then you say you saw Tom Bonnard race off all steamed up. Maybe he was going somewhere anyway, and what you'd said to him hadn't a damn thing to do with it," Alcott theorized.

"Too many coincidences," Fargo countered. "First they insisted I was wrong. Then they came up with explanations, and none of them holds up. They're hiding something, I tell you, Joe."

Alcott shook his head in puzzlement as he sent his horse forward. "I'm going to look through every damn scrap of paper in my files about the Bonnards. Maybe I'll find something that'll help explain this. Meanwhile, what about these patrols? They're not getting us any further than Roy Guiness's did."

"See you tomorrow night," Fargo answered, and rode on until he reached the black locust. It had become a comfortable place to bed down, and as he stretched out, Joe Alcott's words stayed with him. It was true, the patrols had produced nothing, and that didn't add up, either. In order to seize young women for the slave trade, somebody had to lie in wait. They had to be there along the roads or the riverbank. At best, they had to watch and wait just back of the roads. In any case they had to be close enough to see and be seen. But there had been nothing except the stabbing uneasiness that rode with him. If another few nights of patrolling brought nothing more, he'd have to come up with something else. He turned on his side, swore softly, and let sleep shut out further thoughts.

He slept soundly, and the morning was humid, with a thick haze that the sun burned away before he'd finished washing in the stream. He decided to go over the road in the daylight to see if he might spot something he'd missed by night. It was clutching at straws, he realized as he slowly rode across the thick green fields until he reached the first road. He sent the pinto down the road, retraced steps, thoroughly scanning the narrow roadway and low brush. When he finished, he did the same with the second road, and finally traversed the riverbank.

The day had slid into the afternoon when he finally finished, and he rode away with a furrow dug deep across his brow. He had seen nothing more than what he'd observed by night—low brush cover, hardly tall enough to hide a man much less a horse, and behind that, mostly flatland. Tree cover didn't start until too far beyond the roads to afford a clear view, especially at night. By day, the brush beside the roads seemed even more impossible to be a haven for a band of bushwhackers. He rode back across the thick grass fields dissatisfied. He felt as if he were watching a stage set in which none of the pieces seemed to fit in the proper place.

He'd ridden back toward the black locust, almost by habit now, when he spied Gail on the dark-sable standardbred come across the field toward him. She wore an off-white shirt over her tan riding britches, managing to look both tailored and cool and very feminine.

"Been looking for you," she said as she dismounted. He swung down from the Ovaro to stand before her as her gray eyes searched his face. "I want to talk," she said.

"Think up any more explanations?" he slid at her, and saw the gray eyes flare at once.

"That's not fair," she snapped. He half-shrugged and waited. "I thought you might have the good manners to listen with an open mind," she said.

"I'm here. Talk," he grunted.

"If anything did happen to you at Dark Willows, we weren't there. That's easy enough to check out. That means neither Tom nor I were involved in it. It's unfair of you to keep implying anything different," she said.

"You come out here just to tell me I hurt your feelings?" Fargo drawled.

Gail's lips tightened. "No, dammit. I came to tell you to get on with the real reason you're here, finding the answer to those kidnappings. Don't waste your time and energy on this. It's over and you survived. Forget about it, whatever it was."

"Can't do that," Fargo said calmly. "I was almost killed and left for dead. That makes me very irritable."

"It seems to me you're more interested in finding trouble than doing what you came here to do," Gail threw back. "I heard about you and Jeremy. He's really out to get even with you. I can tell him to back off. He'll listen to me."

"If I back off everything else. A little deal?" Fargo questioned.

"Not a deal. An exchange of common-sense behavior," she snapped.

"Sorry," Fargo said.

"I don't understand you." She frowned. "Yesterday at the lake you'd have made love to me if I'd let you."

"Maybe." He grinned.

"No maybe about it. Even though you seem convinced that I'm involved in what happened to you, you'd make love to me," she said.

"I figured maybe you'd lay better than you lie," Fargo said.

"Bastard," Gail hissed, and swung a blow at his face. He caught her arm, half-spun her around, and stepped back a half-pace. Gail's eyes shot gray fire at him. "It was a mistake coming to talk to you, a waste of time," she said.

"I wouldn't want you to think that," Fargo said, and reached out, pulled her to him, and smothered her mouth with his. He pressed hard, forced her lips open, and let his tongue dart forward. He felt her lips soften, press back, quiver, before she tore away from him. "Now it wasn't a waste of time for you." Fargo grinned.

Gail Bonnard, fury in her face, backed to her horse, spun, and flung herself into the saddle. She raced away, and he watched her go until she was out of sight in the dusk. He sank down on the grass and stretched out. His thoughts stayed on Gail Bonnard. She had come with a sincere proposition, yet there had been a note of desperateness to it.

Why? he wondered. She and Tom had first denied everything, then insisted he was mistaken, and finally came up with a story to explain everything away. Now Gail had come and tried to be reasonable first, then bargain for his backing off. What did the sadistic little blonde and the giant hulk mean to her? A frown dug into his brow as he let thoughts develop. Maybe they didn't mean a damn thing to her, Fargo thought as he recalled the edge of helpless pleading he'd caught in her voice. Maybe it was her brother she was trying to protect. He turned the thought slowly. It was entirely possible. Tom Bonnard had been visibly upset over talk of the little blonde. Gail would have to support him. Blood, family, heritage, position—everything dictated that. Tom Bonnard was running for state senator. Maybe he'd been playing with the kind of girls he wouldn't want the voters to know about.

Fargo closed his eyes as dark dropped over the countryside. Speculating was fruitless. He still had to find the little blonde for answers. He stretched and half-dozed until it was time to meet Joe Alcott and Bill Howes.

Low clouds scudded across the sky as he rode over the thick grass of the fields, reached their usual meeting place at the first road, and waited.

Bill Howes appeared a few minutes later and halted beside him. "Joe's late," he remarked after a few minutes more of waiting.

Fargo peered across the flatland but saw no horseman come into sight under the dim moonlight.

"Not like him," Bill Howes said after another ten minutes had gone by.

"He told me he was going to pore through all his files. Maybe he just missed the time," Fargo said.

"Not Joe. He lives with time and deadlines for that newspaper of his," the man answered, and Fargo felt a stab of uneasiness. He glanced at the moon, let another fifteen minutes go by, and swung the Ovaro around.

"Something's wrong. Let's go see," he grunted.

"He's been real tired lately, I know that," Bill said as they set off across the fields at a fast trot. "Could be he just plumb fell asleep, though that's not like him, either."

"We'll find out," Fargo said.

They stayed at a fast trot over the flatland, came to

the road that led into St. Lucifer, and turned their horses down the narrow path as Fargo's eyes scanned the darkness. "He'd have come this way to meet us?" he asked, and Bill nodded gravely. Fargo put the pinto into a gallop for the last mile into the town, slowing only as he entered the main street.

St. Lucifer was darkened, a mostly sleeping town except for the tinny sound of a piano that drifted into the night from the dance hall. The wide window of the newspaper office appeared, and Fargo halted, dismounted, and stepped to the door. He saw Bill go around the side of the building as he opened the door and peered into the darkness inside. "Joe, you in here?" he called. Only silence answered.

"His horse is out back," Fargo heard Bill call as he came up behind him. Fargo drew the big Colt from its holster as he pushed the door open wider. A shaft of dim moonlight drifted into the big room. The long worktable dimly took shape, and behind it loomed the black bulk of the printing press. Fargo peered into the workshop-office, discerned fonts of type and a kerosene lamp on the long table. He stepped to the end of the table, turned the lamp up, and its soft yellow glow spread across the room.

"He's not here," he heard Bill mutter.

Fargo started to agree when he paused, his eyes on the old wooden desk. Papers and file folders were strewn across the top of the desk and on the floor, and he saw an ashtray overturned, a pipe and tobacco scattered over the papers. His brows drew together as he stepped behind the long worktable and stumbled, almost fell over the figure on the floor.

"Damn," Fargo said as he dropped to one knee beside Joe Alcott. The man's left arm was twisted brokenly half under him, a long gash across his forehead. Fargo leaned forward to the still figure. The man was breathing, he found, and he turned his head to call to Bill Howes when the voice growled.

"Don't anybody move," it said. "Drop the gun, big boy."

Fargo looked up and saw the man rise from behind the press, a heavy Walker Colt in his hand. Two more figures rose up from in back of the press, and a fourth man moved into sight near the door.

"Drop it," the man barked out. He had a coarse, heavy face with a reddened, heavy-drinker's complexion.

Fargo eyed the man's gun and decided it was too close and too dead on him. Even a poor shot couldn't miss from where he stood. He let his own Colt drop from his fingers to the floor, and the man stepped forward at once. Fargo saw the man's right leg lift, the kick lash out at his head. The man had aimed low, expecting him to try to duck away, but Fargo flung himself forward, taking the force of the boot against his chest. He wrapped one arm around the leg and yanked. The man went down onto his back, his shots going up into the ceiling, and Fargo heard the volley of gunshots erupt from the other side of the table. He felt a shower of wood chips as bullets tore into the table over his head.

A stray shot hit the lamp and plunged the room into instant darkness. He heard shouts of pain, curses, and more gunfire, caught Bill Howes' voice as the man yanked his leg back, half-rolled, and came up firing. But Fargo had flattened himself on the floor, and the bullets grazed his back. His hand groped to find his Colt, closed around it. He brought the gun around, fired from his prone position, and heard the man's gargled, gasped oath of pain as both shots thudded into him. Fargo rose on one knee, peered over the top of the table. The explosion of shots had subsided, but the others were still in the room, he was certain.

"Son of a bitch. You're a dead man," a voice roared out in confirmation. Fargo's hand brushed against a half-dozen pieces of lead type atop the table. He picked them up, tossed them half across the floor, where they landed with a loud clatter. His Colt was raised and ready as the two figures rose from the other end of the press and poured gunfire in the direction of the noise. He fired and both figures toppled forward, fell to the floor, and lay still.

Fargo waited, listened. There'd been a fourth man, and he half-spun as the figure dived from the far wall and sailed out of the door. The Trailsman raced from behind the table, holstered the Colt as he ran. He wanted that one alive, able to answer questions. He darted through the door to see the man pulling himself onto a horse. He vaulted atop the Ovaro as the fleeing bushwhacker raced down the dark, wide street.

Fargo sent the powerful pinto charging after the man and saw his quarry turn in the saddle, fire off two shots that were wide of the mark. He flattened himself onto the Ovaro's neck as the man fired two more shots, closer to their target this time.

But Fargo let the Ovaro continue to close in fast on the other horse and slung himself to the side of the pinto as the man fired a shot that whistled across the top of the saddle. Fargo clung for a moment, pulled his head up, and saw the Ovaro was almost abreast of the other horse. The fleeing bushwhacker fired again, in fear and desperation this time, and the shot was high and wide. That was the sixth shot, and the man had no time to reload.

Fargo pulled himself back into the saddle, sent the Ovaro veering into the other horse, and dived at his quarry. The man tried to duck away, but Fargo's long arms locked around him, and he flew from the racing horse, Fargo clinging to him. Both figures hit the ground, Fargo landing half on his side, the man on his back. Fargo was on his feet first, and he reached down and yanked the man up. He sent a sharp right whistling into the man's belly, and the man doubled over, fell onto his knees, his head down. Fargo smashed him backhanded across the face, and he sprawled backward on the ground.

"Now you're going to talk, mister. Who sent you?" Fargo rasped. He let the man roll onto his side, both his hands still clutching his midsection as he sucked in deep gasps of air.

"Wait. I can't breathe," the man gasped.

Fargo allowed him another half-minute. "You've got enough breath back. Talk," he growled as he reached down and grasped the man by the shoulder.

The man still had his hands clutched to his abdomen, but he suddenly drew them away, and Fargo caught the flash of the knife blade as it whipped upward through the air. He let go of the man's shoulder and half-fell, half-flung himself backward. His heel hit something on the ground, and he went down as he saw the man, knife blade upraised, dive at him. Fargo got his arms up, caught the man's wrist with one hand, lifted his knee, and brought it up into the diving figure's chest. The man catapulted over his head.

Fargo whirled and regained his feet as the figure slammed into the ground, and he drew the Colt. "Drop the knife," he ordered. But the figure lay unmoving. Fargo took a step closer, felt his lips draw back in anger and disgust. He half-circled the figure and saw the knife protruding from the man's abdomen just under the point of his rib cage. He dropped to one knee, pulled the figure onto its back, and the man's eyes stared at him with the horror of pain and death in their depths.

"Who sent you, dammit?" Fargo asked. The man's lips moved but no sound came from them. Fargo started to lean closer as he saw the last flicker of life leave the staring eyes. The figure sagged into death and Fargo cursed softly as he stood up, turned to where the Ovaro had trotted back.

He climbed onto the horse and cantered back to St. Lucifer to see a small crowd outside the newspaper office. He dismounted as two men came out carrying Bill Howes' lifeless form.

"Goddamn," Fargo bit out. "Where's Joe Alcott?"

"He was taken to Doc Tillis down the street," one of the men said. "Who're you?"

"Skye Fargo. I was working with Joe. I chased one of them who ran," Fargo answered. "He's dead up the road a piece."

"We'll send someone out there," the man said.

Fargo nodded, took the Ovaro by the reins, and walked along the street until he came to the frame house with lights burning brightly. He knocked on the door, and a young man in shirt sleeves answered.

"Doc Tillis," Fargo said. "I was with Joe Alcott." The young man opened the door wider and Fargo stepped into the house, saw a living room to one side, two more rooms down a hallway.

"In here," the young man said. "I'm Doc Tillis' assistant." Fargo followed him into the first room, where a tall thin man wearing a white jacket looked up from a table where he was laying out a splint and bandages. "Friend of Joe Alcott's," the young man said.

"How is he?" Fargo asked.

"Gash on the head isn't too bad. But they broke his arm. I'm going to set it in a minute," the doctor said.

"Can I see him?" Fargo asked.

"Better do it now before I set his arm," the doctor said. "Next room. Don't be long."

Fargo nodded and hurried into the next room to see Joe Alcott stretched out on a low table with a white-sheeted mattress on it. His head had already been bandaged, and Fargo saw the pain in his face as he turned to see him. "What did they want, Joe? Why'd they attack you?" Fargo asked.

"They wanted to find you. I told them I didn't know where you were, but they wouldn't believe me," the man said, his voice drained. "They kept on beating on me."

"They say who sent them?" Fargo questioned.

"No. I asked that and they slugged me again. Hired killers, Fargo. Their kind's easy to come by if you've the money to buy them," Joe Alcott said, and winced in pain. "But it was you they were after."

Fargo turned as the doctor and his young assistant entered the room with a tray of medical equipment. He cast another glance at Joe Alcott's worn, pain-racked face and decided to say nothing about Bill Howes' death. That news could wait another twenty-four hours.

"I'll come by tomorrow, Joe," he said, and walked from the room, the muscles in his jaw throbbing. He paused outside to rest one hand on the Ovaro's neck. Hired killers sent to find him and kill him, he muttered. Hired by whom? The question dangled before him. In other places the list might be long and made up of anything from old grudges to old flames. But here the list was short, with only two names on it: Tom Bonnard and Jeremy Tallant.

Fargo pulled himself onto the horse and rode

slowly out of St. Lucifer as he turned both names in his mind. Jeremy Tallant was a bad loser. He'd proved that at the race. He was mean-minded enough, the kind who couldn't stand losing face, especially in front of a woman. He might even talk himself into thinking he was acting to protect Gail, and he was the type who'd pay others to do what he hadn't the stomach for himself. But he still saw Tallant as a snobbish damn fool without the kind of guts it took to hire killers. Yet he wasn't ready to rule out the man.

He turned his thoughts to Tom Bonnard. The man was essentially an unknown quantity. He had the power and money to hire killers. Did he have the fear to make him do it? The question hung unanswered as he reached the black locust and bedded down. There'd be no patrolling this night. If anything were to happen, it had occurred already as the moon moved toward the horizon.

Fargo closed his eyes and welcomed sleep. The night had turned sour, and he was glad to let it pass on. He slept heavily until morning came to wake him with a high haze that burned away quickly to become a scorching sky before midmorning. The questions of the night returned with stabbing insistence, and he searched his mind as he again breakfasted on plums and pecans. But he found nothing that gave any answers.

He saddled up slowly and started to ride back to St. Lucifer. Bitter anger hung around him as an invisible cloak. The reasons that had brought him down here were still there—still as far away from being solved as ever. Furthermore, one man had died, and another almost, because of him. He spat angrily and knew the heaviness of guilt.

He reached the town with his lips drawn tight and

reined up outside the doctor's house. The man emerged before he had a chance to dismount. "You'll find him at the office," Doc Tillis said.

"What?" Fargo frowned.

"His arm's in a splint, and he has it in a sling. I couldn't keep him here," Doc Tillis explained, and Fargo shook his head in disbelief as he rode on to the newspaper office. The door was open, and he dismounted and strode in to see Joe Alcott behind the battered desk, his left arm in a shoulder sling.

"What are you trying to prove?" Fargo asked.

"Got work to do. They told me about Bill," Joe said, his sensitive face drawn.

Fargo slumped into the chair by the desk. "Stinkin' lousy," he bit out. "My fault, all of it."

"Can't say that. The dice fell the wrong way," Joe said.

"Maybe if I'd backed off, they wouldn't have been sent to get me," Fargo returned bitterly.

"A man does what he has to do," Joe Alcott said. "Maybe you're onto more than you know."

"Maybe, or maybe it was just a gutless bastard who couldn't stand losing," Fargo said. "But I'll find out, for more reasons than before."

"It'll be just the two of us tonight," Joe said.

"Hell, Joe, you're in no shape to patrol," Fargo protested.

"I don't need two hands to ride, and I can watch, and come get you. That's what you said you wanted anyway," the man answered. Fargo read Joe Alcott's drawn face and saw as much inner pain as outer reflected there. Riding patrol was Joe Alcott's way of striking back, of feeling less helpless. He wouldn't take that from him.

"So I did," Fargo murmured. "Get some rest before tonight." He pushed himself out of the chair and left the office. Outside, he led the Ovaro to the town blacksmith, had him check the horse's hooves. He waited as the man tightened one on the right forefoot and then walked the horse down the main street by the cheek strap. He noticed the dark-green ladies' stanhope in front of the general store. He had just started past the elegant little rig when he saw Gail emerge from the store, the shopkeeper behind her with three full bags of groceries. She saw him and came around to the other side of the stanhope as the shopkeeper put the bags into the carriage.

"I heard. News gets around fast," she said. "I'm sorry."

"Got anything better than that?" Fargo growled.

"I don't know who was behind it, if that's what you mean," she said.

"Don't know or don't want to know?" he growled.

"Don't know. I was sick when I heard about it because I knew what you'd think. But you're wrong. It had to be someone who knew why you were here to begin with, and wanted to stop you before you found out anything," Gail said. "And I am sorry, terribly sorry over it."

He searched the gray eyes. She meant her words, or she was one damn good actress, he murmured inwardly. He wasn't about to decide which yet.

"Somebody hired those bushwhacking bastards. Somebody will pay for it," he growled as he turned and led the horse on, feeling her eyes following him. He swung onto the Ovaro after a while and rode out of town, turned, and made a wide circle that brought him behind the stanhope as Gail drove from St. Lucifer. He hung back and followed, the carriage a tiny spot in the distance. She made no detours, he saw, and drove directly to the big house. He pulled up under a cluster of thick black willows and watched as she entered the house, a servant bringing the groceries in after her.

Fargo stayed under the trees, his eyes on the house, and in time he saw Tom Bonnard emerge, go into the stable, and bring out a gray Arabian. He exercised the horse in one of the corrals, put the mount through a dozen jumps, and returned it to the stable. Fargo continued to watch as Tom Bonnard came out and went back into the main house. He didn't reappear, and as the day wore on, Fargo left the trees and rode the countryside. His eyes swept every stand of trees, every hollow, every shallow glen. He looked for a cluster of horsemen, or even a single rider, anyone that seemed to wait in silent patience. But he saw no one.

At the far end of his circle he neared the thick line of weeping willows and beyond them, the beginning of the cypresses that marked the bayous, and he thought about Nannine. She'd been the only good thing that had happened to him since he'd come here, and he made a mental note to pay her another visit before he left.

The day had started to wear down, and he rode slowly through the dusk, continued on as the dark night followed to swallow the flat grassy fields. As the pale moonlight sent its tentative fingers across the land, he reached the first of the two roads and waited. He saw Joe Alcott come into sight, riding slowly, He studied the man's face as Joe pulled to a halt and saw as much determination as pain.

"We'll ride the riverbank tomorrow night," he said, and Joe nodded and turned his horse down the road. Fargo went on to the other roadway and put the Ovaro into a slow trot. Once again he scanned the low brush as he rode down the center of the road, and once again he felt the uneasiness wrap itself around him. He was not alone, dammit, he swore, yet he saw no one. He had to wonder if perhaps his imagination was running away with him. He cast the thought aside angrily. There was something, somewhere, someplace, cloaked in the dark of the night, and his gaze scanned the flatland beyond the roadsides. He cursed at the emptiness he saw there. He peered at a clump of chestnuts, sought the dark outline of a horse and rider, found nothing, and rode on.

He'd made one sweep south along the road, retraced steps northward, patrolled the narrow lane back again as the hours wore on. He had reached the southern end of his patrol area, turned back, and had gone a little over a mile north when he saw the dark shape ahead of him. He spurred the Ovaro into a canter, and the dark shape became an open-topped Brunswick. The carriage was halted in the middle of the road, the horse standing quietly. Fargo reined to a halt as he reached the two-seated carriage and saw the driver, reins still clutched in one hand, lying across the front seat, his eyes open and staring, his throat slashed from ear to ear and red still pouring from the thin cut.

"Goddamn," Fargo swore as he leapt down from the saddle. He yanked his Colt out and fired three shots into the air as his eyes swept the surrounding terrain. He saw nothing and spun back to the wagon, peering into the rear of it. A woman's shoe lay on the floor, and he saw a piece of cotton blouse hanging from the door handle where it had been ripped away. The sound of a horse galloping came to him, and his hand was on the butt of the big Colt when he saw Joe Alcott appear.

"Shit," the man muttered as he came to a halt, slowly letting himself down from his horse. "You see it happen?" he asked.

"No," Fargo said. "But I was this way less than an hour ago. There was nobody in the brush. I'd have seen them, or anybody holed up nearby. Goddamn, I'd have seen them," he swore bitterly. He spun, dropped to one knee, and swept the ground beside the carriage. The marks and prints became what letters and words were to other men.

"Two girls, dragged out, dragged across the road," he said, and felt the frown dig hard into his forehead. "Three, maybe four attackers. Funny damn prints," he muttered. "Close together, like they hopped around a lot." He stared at the prints, rose to his feet, and followed the tracks. "They dragged the girls through the brush here, across the field on the other side," he said.

"They had to have been hiding in the brush to jump the carriage when it passed," Joe said.

"I'd have seen them, goddammit," Fargo flung back in angry frustration. "Even without horses I'd have seen them." He whirled, took the Ovaro's reins, and led the horse as he started to follow the tracks. The grass was still pressed down where they had dragged the two young women.

"No signs of a struggle. They probably knocked the girls out," he said. He moved carefully after the tracks under the pale moonlight and continued to shake his head in disbelief. He'd followed some hundred yards or more when he slowed, his eyes peering at the thick grass. "They stopped here," he said, knelt down again to scan the area. "Picked up somebody else," he said, and pointed to two large footprints still visible in the thick grass. "The girls were carried from here," he said as the drag marks disappeared. The sets of close-together footprints grew fainter, but the large, new prints were clear in the thick grass.

Fargo followed, Joe Alcott beside him, and the set

of large footprints stayed clear while the others vanished and suddenly reappeared at a place of soft earth, then grew unreadable again. "They turned here," Fargo said as the one set of prints veered to the left, moved along near a shallow stream.

"They must've come a half a mile from the road by now," Joe said, and Fargo nodded, walked in a half-crouch as he peered at the dew-wet grass, which was springing back into place too quickly. But the one set of prints led to a small cluster of smooth sumac, and Fargo followed the trail to the trees, halted as he knelt down again.

"They picked up horses here, three of them," he said, his eyes following the marks on the ground. "They headed south." He mounted the Ovaro, waited while Joe painfully pulled himself into the saddle, and followed the tracks that were still fresh in the thick grass. The moon had dipped low in the sky, and only a pale glow touched the land. Fargo bent low in the saddle as he followed the trail. It led straight, barely visible enough to see, but he managed to keep hold of it until suddenly a line of heavy weeping willows rose up in front of him, and just beyond them the twisted cypresses. The hoofprints led into the willows, on into the black tangle of the dense cypresses.

"The bayous," Joe Alcott said, drawing to a halt beside him. "We can't go in there, not even on foot much less on horseback."

"They went in," Fargo said.

"They know their way in, obviously," Joe said. "And I'd wager they left their horses someplace just beyond that first line of cypresses."

Fargo cursed softly as he peered into the inky blackness of the dense foliage. He'd never pick up a trail in that stygian land, maybe not even by day. He grimaced as he remembered the tortuous tangle of pathways Nannine had led him on as she took him from her little hut. He backed the Ovaro a half-dozen paces, swept the line of willows with his eyes. "Got any idea what part of the bayous this is?" he asked Joe.

"None," Joe said, and followed as Fargo turned the horse and moved north along the edge of the line of willows. It had to be close to where Nannine had led him out, he was certain. He had come out near the north end of the line of trees, he remembered, and he felt sure he could find the place by day. He turned off after they'd gone a quarter-mile or so, and halted when they reached the road to St. Lucifer.

"You go on home, Joe," Fargo said. "I'll check in with you tomorrow. Maybe somebody will have asked about a carriage and some girls that never arrived."

"I'll send Feeny, the undertaker, out to take care of that poor devil in the stanhope," Joe said as he watched Fargo stare into the night with eyes narrowed. "What're you thinking?" he asked.

"I'm thinking it just doesn't figure, dammit. They had to be waiting by the roadside, only they weren't. I would've seen them, only I didn't. Goddammit, it doesn't figure," he bit out.

Joe Alcott shrugged helplessly. "Got no answers either," he said as he sent the horse down the road.

Fargo struck out across the fields, headed back to the black locust that had become his nightly home. But the events of the night rode with him, accusing, mocking, taunting, and when he finally stretched out, he found himself thinking of the trail that had led to the bayous. Nannine swam into his thoughts. He remembered how she had refused to go beyond the two arched cypresses they had seen.

115

"The devil lives there," she had said. "Sometimes at night there is strange singing and sometimes screams. The devil's music." Old legends, superstition, and romantic mysticism, he had told himself. But maybe not, he frowned now. Maybe a lot more real than legends and superstitions. He had to find his way back to Nannine, Fargo vowed, and he turned onto his side.

The Bonnards and sadistic little blondes would be set aside now, suddenly unimportant. He forced himself to sleep as dawn stole over the horizon, and he stayed asleep until his body gathered itself into waking at midmorning.

When he'd washed and dressed, he rode directly to St. Lucifer and the newspaper office.

Joe Alcott met him at the door, drawn tiredness still in his face. "You were right. Two girls," Joe said. "Man named Hobson came asking if anyone knew why his daughter, May, and her friend Valerie hadn't arrived. They were being driven from up north in a stanhope."

Fargo's face was grim. "You tell him we followed a trail?" he asked.

"No. I thought it best not to get his hopes up until we had more than we do now," Joe said, and Fargo nodded agreement. "What happens next?" Joe queried.

"I'm going into the bayous after them," Fargo said.

"Alone?" Joe frowned.

"It's the only way. If they're hiding out there, as it seems, a posse bulling their way through wouldn't get anywhere near without setting them hightailing it," Fargo answered.

"You'll never find them. You'll get yourself sucked into a swamp or eaten by a gator. You don't know your way in there," Joe said.

"I aim to have help," Fargo said.

"That girl you told me about?" Joe asked, and Fargo nodded. "You can get yourself killed just trying to find her." Joe frowned.

"Got to try," Fargo said.

"If you find them, what then?" Joe pressed.

"I come back for help. Once I pin down where they're hiding out, we can move in on them," Fargo said.

"Good luck. You'll need it, friend," Joe Alcott said.

"Keep the faith," Fargo said as he wheeled the Ovaro and rode away. He began to pull on the mental notes he'd made when Nannine had led him from the bayous. He swung left after he was out of town. He put the Ovaro into a fast trot and rode until he spotted the long line of thick weeping willows that bordered the green flatland. He swerved to the edge of the trees and continued on, slowing the horse as his eyes searched the land ahead. Suddenly he reined up as he spotted the mark he sought, the tall rock with a wide willow on each side of it. He had come out of the dense, tangled bayou foliage there. He turned the horse left and headed through the willows.

He rode slowly, carefully, the hanging willow fronds brushing against his face as he moved through the trees. A few cypresses came into view, but he ignored them as he searched for the next mark he'd fastened in his mind. Finally he saw it and turned left again where the swamp of fungus-covered, dead tree stumps stretched out. He moved alongside the mordant swamp. The pinto's ears flattened, flicked forward, flattened again. The horse was becoming nervous as he felt the ground grow soft under his hooves and smelled the dark, dank odor of swampland. With true horse sense he immediately knew the feel and the scent of land that spelled danger for him.

Fargo spotted a huge willow with a large patch of ground where silver nightshade grew on firm soil. He took the horse over to it, dismounted, tethered the animal on a long lead that gave him freedom to roam the entire path beside the willow. It'd give him ample grazing and room to move about until he returned, Fargo observed with satisfaction, and moved away on foot. He crossed back to the semisoft ground alongside the swamp dotted with tree stumps.

He made his way along the swamp until it came to an end and the tangle of foliage grew thicker. He halted, peered into the trees until he spotted the single row of pond cypresses mixed in with black willows. He set out again, his eyes keeping the line of trees in his vision as he carefully picked his way along the ground where the swamp ferns grew ever larger and thicker. Finally he saw the next natural signpost he'd etched into his mind: a trio of bent cypresses. Nannine had turned there, and he did so, too, but each step slow, now, testing the ground ahead before putting his feet down firmly. The swampland was made of deadly, sucking pits that were hidden in patches under the lush vegetation, he saw. But he was quickly learning the particular growths that marked the soft, sucking areas—the dark-green ferns thicker, heavier, shinier; the presence of the cinnabar-red water lily.

He continued to move on with painstaking slowness, aware that one hasty misstep could plunge him into sucking death. The dank, humid heat grew heavier, and he felt little beads of perspiration clinging to his skin. As the hours passed, the scent of hyacinth grew stronger, mixed in with the faint odor of mimosa. He realized that the sense of smell had its own memory. He felt the surge of excitement course through him as he espied the last landmark he sought: the red mangroves. He was getting close to where Nannine had taken him from her cabin, but he forced himself to move slowly, the chance of a fatal misstep still very real.

He saw the dense mangrove thicket where the red ones ended. Testing the ground, he climbed through the thick tangle of roots, tendrils, hanging moss, and trailing vines. He recognized the damp odor of still water now. He had just clambered over a thick pile of roots when, through the hanging moss, he saw the little cabin. Nannine was on the warped little dock in the short brown shift, staring into the thicket. She had obviously heard his approach, and hands on hips, she waited with a frown that turned into amazement as she saw him appear.

"Fargo," she shouted, and ran toward him as he pushed out of the thicket. She flung herself into his arms, and he held her lithe, young body, her high breasts digging into his chest as her black hair cascaded around his shoulders. "You come back to Nannine," she chortled.

"Sort of," he said, and returned her kiss as she pressed her mouth on his.

She pulled back, and her black eyes searched his face. "You are well," she said, an approving comment.

"I am well." He laughed. "Surprised I found my way back?"

"Stupéfaite!" she said.

"I came because I need your help," he told her. "I need you to show me the way back to that part of the bayou where you said the devil lives. You remember?"

"Oui," Nannine said, a tiny frown touching her smooth, sepia brow. "Why?"

"I think someone hides in there," he said.

"*Le diable* hides there. I will not go in there," she told him. "You should not, either."

"I must. I must see for myself," he said.

"*Démence*," she muttered darkly.

"Can you get me a pirogue?" he asked.

"Christophe's pirogue is here," Nannine said. "You want to go now?"

"No, after it gets dark," Fargo said, and watched the little smile edge Nannine's sharply etched lips.

"It will not be dark for an hour at least," she said as her arms slid around his neck.

"Lots of time," Fargo agreed as Nannine's mouth lifted to his. Her lips pressed hard, and he felt the tip of her tongue slide out, draw back. She stepped away, turned, and led him into the little cabin where she spun lightly, crossed her arms, and pulled the shift over her head in one fluid motion.

Fargo stared, her sepia beauty even more striking than he'd remembered as she stood before him with natural, unaffected pride. She displayed her lean, lithe body, high sharp breasts, and flat little belly.

He quickly shed gun belt and clothes, Nannine's eyes following his every move, watching the rising, swelling shaft that reached out for her. He stepped toward her and she dropped to her knees, her arms encircling his legs, hands pressing hard into his buttocks as she drew him to her. Her face pressed against him, her lips parted, searching, groping to find him and close around him. He heard her little gasp of pleasure as she caressed with her lips. Nannine cooed as she pulled, stroked, kissed, sucked, and caressed his shaft. Her soft, wet lips wrapped deliciously around him, and he sank down with her as she fell back onto the mattress on the floor, never taking her lips from him. She sank lower, her hands rubbing across his belly, and he heard his own voice join her little gasped sounds of pleasure.

Nannine rubbed as she clung, her cooing sounds of delight growing deeper, throatier, and he felt the ecstasy gather inside him, spiral quickly to carry him with it as Nannine's lips tightened, pulled, grew even more full of intense pleasure. Ecstasy raced upward, his hips lifted as the spiral of pleasure exploded, and he heard his own groan mingle with Nannine's. "Oh, God," he moaned as she continued, enveloping him with the delicious, warm wetness of her caresses until finally he fell back limply, the instant exhaustion of passion consumed, followed by the wonderful weakness that was its own pleasure.

Nannine pulled herself up, cradled herself against his chest, and he cupped a hand around one firm, pointed breast. "I have thought about your return, Fargo," she murmured. "I hoped, but I did not believe it would happen. But you are here. It is better than before." She drew one leg up and over his pelvis and slowly began to rub up and down along his thick, curly tangle, up over his belly, her lean, smooth leg moving down over his thigh with insinuating slowness.

He felt himself responding almost at once, beginning to rise, palpitate, thicken. Nannine rubbed her leg over him, felt the hardness of him rising, and he heard her gasp of excitement. He half-rose, rolled over with her, pressed himself over her lean, coffee-and-milk loveliness. Her legs came open, rose, folded around him at once, and she thrust upward, dark-fire welcome. She gave a tiny scream as he entered her with smooth, sliding fullness.

"Fargo, mon chéri. J'ai besoin de toi ... j'ai besoin de toi," she said breathlessly, and he felt her fingers dig into the small of his back. The urgency filled her, reached out to him as she pushed, quivered, cried out, the flesh demanding, passion racing away with itself. He responded, dug deep and hard, increased speed as Nannine's cries became tiny yelps of desire. His mouth fell upon her firm, upturned breasts, and he drew first one, then the other into his mouth as he pumped and thrust, letting his lips suck in rhythm with his momentum.

He felt Nannine's body tense, her passion begin to reach upward to that moment of moments, and he pushed harder, faster as she cried out, cried out again. Yet she somehow managed to hold back, letting ecstasy continue to build inside her. "Ah, yes, oh, mon Dieu," she murmured, words that were tiny gasps of pleasure. He drove as hard as he could into her and heard her half-scream, half-laugh as she somehow kept herself on the delicious edge of culmination. Her legs tightened around him, her pelvis pushing hard against him, and the lean, lithe sepia form quivered against him, her smooth skin moist with perspiration. Suddenly her efforts crumbled under the demands of the body, passion shattering willpower, the senses refusing to be denied any longer. Nannine screamed, and her head fell back, black hair whipping wildly from side to side as the climax swept over her with devouring vehemence, and her fingers clawed against Fargo's back. The absolute, frenzied wildness of her swept him along, and he came with her as her screams filled the little cabin. He stayed with her, continued to thrust until the flesh succumbed to the too-quick extinction of passion, and he slid down beside her as she groaned in matching fulfillment.

She came against him, arms around his chest, and slept at once. He closed his eyes and let the warm slumber of satisfaction wrap itself around him as well. He woke later. The little cabin was dark, and he pushed up on one elbow. Nannine stirred at once and half-rolled to the edge of the mattress. He saw her reach out, and the soft light of a small candle quickly spread across the cabin. She rolled back to him, stretched with feline beauty, and he marveled at the sheer sensuousness of her coffee-and-milk body as it glowed softly in the candlelight.

"It's time," he murmured, and saw her face fall in disappointment. He lifted her to her feet, and she clung to him. "Don't want to go, honey," he told her. "But I have to."

She turned, picked up the brown shift as he began to dress. She put it on as she walked from the cabin, and it was his turn to be disappointed as her sepia beauty disappeared under the garment.

When he finished dressing, he stepped outside to see her in one of the two pirogues beside the dock. He stepped into the other one and almost capsized, and he caught her quick glance of amusement.

"Damn thing's skittish as an unbroken filly," he muttered as he lowered himself into the little craft and managed to stretch his long legs out enough to pick up the paddle. He put the paddle into the water as Nannine sent her pirogue from the dock with a long, silent sweep. He settled himself, tested the short-handled paddle again, and sent the pirogue forward. By the time he'd followed Nannine a few dozen yards down the still, dark waters, he had found the pirogue not too different from a good birchbark canoe, though too small for his bulk.

Nannine sailed a straight line as the moonlight managed to dimly infiltrate the thick overhead of hanging moss and vines. He saw Nannine turn into another bayou and followed, slowed as she brought her pirogue to a halt. He spied the archway formed

123

by the two cypresses. He paddled up to the mouth of the arch as Nannine kept her pirogue still in the water, and a frown slid across his brow as he heard the singsong wail from beyond the archway. The sound rose and fell, was joined by something that sounded faintly like the high yet soft sound of an ocarina. Suddenly a sharp scream tore into the darkness, came again, and then stopped as suddenly as it had exploded. Fargo saw Nannine's quick glance.

"Musique diabolique," she murmured. "Don't go in."

"Have to," he told her, blew a kiss to her as he sent the pirogue under the archway of cypresses. He saw her watch him go with her round eyes grave, her high-planed face unsmiling. She remained on the other side as he paddled silently away and faded from sight in the dark quickly. The bayou grew narrow, and the air hung thickly with the scent of moss and mimosa. He'd gone on another fifty yards when he saw the faint yellow glow through the hanging moss and thick tendrils, and he moved the pirogue slowly forward. The glow grew stronger, became a soft, flickering light, and he sent the pirogue toward it. A curtain of hanging moss parted as he moved through it, and another quickly took its place in front of him. But he could see the light now, and he slowed the little craft and let the forward motion carry it silently through the water. As he passed through another curtain of vines and moss, he saw the glow of light become three large torches set into the ground at the end of long poles.

Behind the torches he saw a wooden house take shape, a larger version of Nannine's cabin with a smaller hut beside it. The two structures were set on what was obviously a solid stretch of land that bordered the bayou. As he stared at the scene, he saw two girls bound to a single, thick stake, a wide dog collar around each one's neck with a chain leading to the stake.

He leaned forward as the pirogue drifted nearer to the torches, and suddenly the music came again from inside the larger cabin. The sound was clear and unmistakenly the reedy, hollow tone of an ocarina. His eyes returned to the two young women as they sat on the ground, hands tied behind their backs, the chain and collar around each of their necks more than strong enough to hold them captive. One girl was dark-haired, attractive, breasts pushing against the torn bodice of her dress. The other, her hair lighter, her body slimmer, sat with a ripped skirt revealing long, thin legs with a red whipmark across one thigh. Both young women stared with shocked, wide eyes.

Fargo let the pirogue drift closer, pass through another curtain fringe of thick, hanging moss and still another. He reached up, took hold of a vine, and halted the little craft's drift. He was but a dozen yards from the cabins, and a mist drifted across the bayou. The burning torches, the flickering light, the mist, the chained girls, and the eerie music from inside the cabins did indeed make the scene seem as though it were from the underworld of the devil.

He was peering at the scene, holding the pirogue from drifting closer, when he caught the movement at the door of the larger cabin. The figure stepped out, came into the wavering torchlight, and Fargo held the gasp in his throat as he recognized the blond hair, the round, pretty face, and the eyes that were made of burning blue even a dozen yards away.

Goddamn, he murmured to himself. Goddamn. The blonde moved forward as he watched; she was wearing the almost-full-length loose garment she had worn that night in the cellar. As he stared transfixed, she lifted her arms, pulled the long garment off, and stood naked under the torchlight. She had a small, slender body, smallish breasts but nicely formed with strangely large, very red nipples on deep-pink circles, a convex little belly, and a tangle of light-brown pubic hair. Her legs were slender enough, and she had a round, fleshy rump that flashed in front of him as she whirled.

The frown stayed on Fargo's face as the little blonde began to move her body in a writhing, sinuous dance to the music that drifted from the cabin. She swayed, whirled, moved her hips from side to side, and Fargo's eyes went to the cabin again as another figure stepped out of the shadows and into the torchlight. It was the hulking, monstrous form, as naked as the girl. Igor moved forward, his huge, muscled body glistening in the light. He moved toward the dancing blonde, and Fargo saw the two chained girls crawl to huddle together at the stake.

Staring in disbelief, Fargo watched the little blonde swirl her naked body around the hulk's towering form as the huge figure halted and remained motionless. The blonde's burning blue eyes seemed to devour him as she brushed against his huge, treelike thighs, and Fargo watched as her hands reached out to caress the giant's abdomen and move down the hulk's legs. Suddenly Fargo's stare grew deeper. Her hands moved lightly over Igor's organ and returned, caressed it again, and moved away, and the giant stayed impassive. Below his heavy, dangling organ there was nothing but hanging bits of skin. "A eunuch," Fargo hissed. "The damn monster's a eunuch."

As he stared, the little blonde danced around Igor again, rubbed her round belly against his thigh, flicked her hands across his organ, and whirled away. It seemed at first as though she were tantalizing him, but as Fargo watched, he realized that she was exciting herself, engaged in the pursuit of self-gratification. Even as he stared, the hulk remained motionless, his shaven head lifted upward as the blonde danced around him, dropped to her knees, rubbed herself against him. She rose, whirled in front of him, and thrust her light-brown pubic mound against his dangling organ. She whirled away at once, but now she brought her hands up and pressed them around her breasts, dancing with herself in a swaying, undulating motion. Slowly, she sank onto the grass almost under the giant, writhed on her back. She lifted her legs and brought both hands down to her crotch. She probed, touched, caressed, and cried out in wavering moans, and still the reedy, hollow music continued.

Fargo's eyes were riveted on the scene of depraved eroticism, but he found his mind racing with thoughts of the carriage and the roadside only twenty-four hours before. The kidnapped girls were there in front of his eyes, the giant and the sadistic blonde with them, the connection beyond denying. Yet there was no way the hulk could have hidden in the low brush of the roadside, Fargo swore inwardly, no damn way. The whole thing was even more impossible to fit. And did the blonde and the giant in front of him mean that somehow, someway, the Bonnards were behind a slave trade? Questions added onto questions, and still no answers. Only one thing stayed certain in his mind: the giant couldn't have hidden by the roadside. No way. That refused to fit, and it kept everything else from fitting in place.

A sharp half-scream of pleasure from the little blonde brought his thoughts back to her, and he saw her roll, rise to her feet as the music ceased. She turned toward the smaller of the two cabins and seemed to wait. Suddenly the questions that tumbled wildly in Fargo's mind were answered, the impossible suddenly explained, all the pieces that had refused to fit falling into place. He stared as the figures came from the cabin. One came first, then a second, then two more—short, squat, misshapen little bodies leaping and hopping across the ground.

"Dwarfs," Fargo murmured. "Four goddamn dwarfs." It was all so clear suddenly, made even more so as the large-headed, squat figures dropped to the ground in front of the naked little blonde to lay prone, barely visible even in the flat grass. The low brush by the roadside had been more than enough to hide their short shapes. Everything was explained now. They were quick, their little bodies capable of furious little leaps. They attacked the carriages, used surprise on top of surprise, and as the first dwarf rose from the grass, Fargo saw the knife in his belt.

Fargo's big frame leaned forward as he peered through the hanging moss. His thoughts were still putting pieces into place when suddenly he felt the pirogue go over. His curse exploded as he was plunged into the water with a splash that sounded like the roar of a waterfall in the stillness. "Shit," he muttered as he surfaced and swung his eyes to the cabins. The blonde had scooped up her long dress and slipped it on as the hulk stepped forward. The four dwarfs hopped excitedly from side to side, and everyone stared at him. Fargo heard the soft swish of water and glanced over to see two knobby gray shapes surface, little yellow eyes blinking as they began to move toward him.

He struck out toward the only place he could reach in time to avoid the gators and saw the strange assortment of figures waiting. Igor stepped forward, the one large-nosed dwarf with the long-bladed knife in his hand hopped excitedly, and the others moved to spread out. He flicked a glance across at the two gators and saw them moving with unhurried inexorableness toward him, and returned his eyes to the shore. Another of the dwarfs had produced a knife, and the hulk's arms were already reaching out to seize him. It was a hell of a choice, he murmured.

6

He threw another glance at the gators and headed toward the shore. He had a few seconds to spare, he decided, and dived under the surface, struck out underwater for the far end of the stretch of ground near the cabins. When he came up, he was only a few feet from his goal, and he increased speed. He had almost reached the firm land when he saw one of the dwarfs spot him, a creature with a flattened nose and pushed-in face. "Damn," Fargo swore as the dwarf gave a high-pitched shout and began to race toward him. The other three followed, moving with astonishing speed in their hopping, almost monkeylike gait.

Fargo pulled himself from the water and saw the naked eunuch lumbering after them. He dropped to one knee, yanked the Colt from its holster, and fired. But the four little forms leapt away in all directions, twisting and rolling. His two shots missed entirely as the dwarfs disappeared into the dark shadows by the cabins. The naked hulk continued to plod toward him, and Fargo leveled the Colt again.

"Igor, stop," he heard the blonde call out as she rushed up, and the giant halted in his tracks. She stopped beside him, her burning blue eyes staring.

"Surprise," Fargo bit out grimly. "Now get the rest of your playmates out here." He caught the sound to his right, half-whirled, glimpsed a hurtling little form, and fired, the shot only grazing the shape that disappeared into the shadows. Another dwarf leapt from almost behind him, and Fargo was about to pull the trigger but held back as the dwarf vanished. He caught the soft rush of air from the other side, tried to duck, but it was too late. He felt the knife blade hit his hand, a grazing blow that slammed across the top of his knuckles. Yet it was enough to send the Colt flying from his grip. He saw the gun hit the ground and skitter away over the mist-wet grass. He started for it and turned as he saw the four leaping forms rush at him.

One of the dwarfs catapulted through the air not unlike a leaping monkey, the short, squat body aimed at the big man's head. Fargo ducked, but the dwarf managed to slam into his shoulders, a cannonball-like bundle of concentrated weight, and Fargo felt himself go backward. He dropped to one knee as the dwarf slipped to the ground. He felt another furious little form crash into his legs and send him down while still another leapt atop him. Cursing, he rolled and dislodged the one half over his head, kicked out, and heard the high-pitched yelp of pain. Regaining his feet, he felt a sharp stab into his side and saw the knife blade flash again as the little figure clung to his leg. He brought the side of his fist down in a hammerlike blow, all his strength behind it. The dwarf emitted a gargled sound as his head was driven down into his neck, and he fell away to lay crumpled on the ground.

Fargo whirled as another little attacker hurtled into him with astounding force. He got one hand around the dwarf's clinging body and tore the short form away, but he fell forward as another leapt onto his back and wrapped short but powerful arms around his neck. Fargo went down on his hands and knees as two more forms leapt on him, one wrapped around his right leg, the other clinging to his left arm. He yelled in pain as he felt teeth sink into his forearm. He rolled sideways in rage, kicking and twisting, and two of the dwarfs fell away. The one clinging around his neck stayed and squeezed harder.

Fargo felt his breath grow tight. He rose to one knee, dived forward in a half-somersault, and felt the heavy little body sail over his head. The dwarf landed on the grass in front of him, and Fargo leapt forward to come down on him with all his weight. But the dwarf twisted away and sprang to his feet, and Fargo spun as a hurtling body barreled into him from the side, reaching for his throat. He whirled, and the dwarf flew from him, and he saw the two other forms leaping at him from each side. Their speed and concentrated power were unbelievable, and he flung himself forward and kicked out. Both hurtling forms slid from his legs. He rolled, came onto his feet, and turned just in time to see the naked giant lunging at him.

Fargo, off balance, swung a hard right that hadn't enough shoulder behind it, and the giant didn't even pause in his lunge. Fargo twisted away as the treelike arm descended, the blow crashing into the small of his back. A surge of searing pain shot through him as he fell forward, his face in the grass. He felt another blow come down onto the back of his neck, and his head exploded in red and purple lights that disappeared into nothingness. He lay prone, the world vanished into a void of blackness.

*　　*　　*

The senses returned reluctantly. He felt coolness against his face, slowly pulled his eyes open, and blinked. The damp grass came into focus against his face, and he lifted his head, gasped out in pain as the back of his neck cracked with the effort. He tried to move his arms and found his wrists were tied together behind his back. He tried to use his legs to roll, and the pain in his back shot through his body. His legs refused to move properly and he glanced down to see his ankles bound together. He drew both legs up, fighting down his back pain, and managed to draw himself into a sitting position. He was but a few feet away from the two girls huddled beside the stake in the ground, their eyes on him full of sympathy and shattered hope.

He lifted his gaze to see Igor standing nearby, clothed in ragged trousers now and the short vest that left most of his mammoth chest bare. Three of the dwarfs were near him, and Fargo saw the little blonde step from the cabin and cross the grass toward him. Her burning blue eyes bored into him as she halted in front of him.

"The man who wants to die twice," she said.

"Who the hell are you?" Fargo rasped.

"Last time with Igor was nothing," she said, ignoring his question. "You have killed one of the little ones. I will let them have you. When they are finished, you will be their size, and you will still be alive. They are experts." He saw the burning blue eyes move up and down his body, linger on the strong, chiseled lines of his face. "Too bad," she murmured. "I might have enjoyed you."

Fargo's thoughts held on her. He had nothing to lose, he told himself. She was plainly twisted, her pretty blond face hiding pure madness. But a twisted eroticism was there inside the madness. "You going to do another little dance for me first?" he asked.

The burning blue eyes widened. "You had been watching for a while, I see," she said.

"You'd be afraid to dance around me," Fargo said. "You'd get the real thing from me." He let out a slow smile as her eyes narrowed. "Only you're afraid of that. You wouldn't be the virgin queen anymore. You prefer eunuchs and dwarfs. You ought to try a real man."

"Pig," she spit out, but he caught the sudden sharp intake of her breath.

"Come see me if you change your mind," he said. "The real thing, baby, hot and warm and all yours." She spun away from him but not before he saw the faint flush of red come into her face. He watched her stride to the cabin, blond hair swinging behind her. His eyes shifted to the three small figures that sat on their haunches at the edge of the water and stared at him. The one with the big nose had his Colt tucked into the waistband of his short trousers, the gun looking out of proportion. The torches were burning low, and as he watched, one burned itself out and the last of the remaining flickering light grew weak. He looked across at the two girls.

"Which of you is May?" he asked, and the slender one nodded. "It's not over yet," he said with more confidence than he felt.

"They're mad, stark raving mad, all of them," the girl murmured, and fell silent as the blonde came out of the cabin, the hulk beside her. He carried a high-sided tin bowl of water and brought it to the two girls.

"Drink," the blonde ordered as he held the bowl to May's lips.

Fargo saw the girl take a half-dozen sips. Valerie did the same as the giant pushed the bowl to her face.

"Can't let the merchandise dry out, eh?" Fargo said, and the blonde's burning eyes stared at him.

"Don't try to crawl away," she said. "There is only swamp behind the cabins and the gators wait in the water."

"Wouldn't think of it. I'm saving myself for you," Fargo answered.

She turned from him, clapped her hands, and three dwarfs rose and followed her toward the cabins. The hulk slowly turned to fall in last in line, and Fargo's glance caught the letters pressed into the side of the tin bowl, a single word: ELDON. He frowned, tucked the word into a corner of his mind, and watched the blonde and the hulk go into the larger cabin, the three dwarfs into the smaller one.

The last of the torches flickered out to plunge the area into darkness. After a few minutes, the dim moonlight began to assert its pale self and outlined the tall cypresses at his back and the still, dark bayou in front of him. The blonde hadn't lied, he realized. There was no place to crawl to, especially bound hand and foot.

"You two awake?" he called to the girls in a whisper.

"Yes," May Hobson said.

"They tell you anything else?" he asked.

"Not directly, but we heard them talking," she said. "They're going to take us to meet some men coming up from Mexico tomorrow."

"Meet them where?" Fargo asked.

"The Texas border, a place called Leadville," the girl said.

Fargo nodded grimly. "They say anything about

135

anyone else helping them, any other names?" he asked.

"No," May Hobson said.

Fargo stared into the night with his lips tight. The blonde was the twisted brains behind all of it. Yet somehow, some way, there was a connection to the Bonnards. But speculation could wait, he muttered silently as he tried to free his wrists. He gave up after a few minutes, the ropes securely tied. He felt the warm stickiness at his side where one of the dwarfs had knifed him, but it was only a flesh wound. The teeth marks in his forearm hurt more. He twisted his body, tried to bring his legs up high enough for his fingers to reach the throwing knife inside the sheath around his calf, but it was imposssible. He straightened his legs out as he felt a cramp seizing his calf muscles and swore silently as his eyes searched the little path of firm ground.

He rolled his way to the side of the stake that held the two girls, pushed himself upward, and pressed his wrist ropes against the wood. He began to rub, hoping for friction to break off enough splinters that would let him saw the bonds loose. But he swore in frustration as he rubbed up and down against the stake. The task would take days, not hours, and he paused to rest as his arm muscles stiffened. He had put his head back against the stake, his gaze idly focused on the water when he snapped his head up.

"Goddamn," he murmured as he saw Nannine halt the pirogue before him. She had righted the other one and pulled it along behind her, he saw. He waited as she stepped to the ground and ran toward him on bare feet, dropped to one knee at his side.

"Knife around my leg," he whispered.

She lifted his trouser and pulled out the narrow, double-edged throwing blade. She severed his ankle ropes first, then the bonds holding his wrists, and he leapt to his feet as he rubbed circulation back into his wrists. He took the knife from her, started to turn to the girls when he glimpsed the short, squat form racing from the second cabin. The dwarf hopped across the ground with his amazing speed and exploded a high-pitched squeal of alarm. Instantly, the two others barreled out of the cabin. Fargo glanced at the girls. There was no time to cut them loose, and no way to escape with them if he did.

"Stay cool. I'll be coming for you," he flung at them as he raced for the pirogues with Nannine.

But the first dwarf, the big-nosed one, had already crossed in front of him, and Fargo saw the little figure pull the big Colt from his waistband. The dwarf raised it to fire, and Fargo dived sideways. The shot went wild, and he rolled, slamming into the short-legged figure as the dwarf tried to fire again. The little man went down but was on his feet again instantly, still trying to bring the big Colt into position. Fargo reached out, curled his hand around one of the short legs, and yanked, and the dwarf went down on his back, the shot going into the air. Fargo held on to the leg, grabbed hold of the other one, and rose to his feet. He swung the squat form in a wide arc, slamming the dwarf into the second one as he rushed forward. He heard the little figure's gasp of pain.

Fargo continued swinging, brought his body around in a shot-putter's arc, whirled around fully once more, and smashed the murderous dwarf against the nearest cypress. When he heard the over-sized skull crack in two against the tree trunk, he dropped his hold and raced after Nannine. A glance at the cabin showed him the blonde running out, rifle in hand, Igor after her.

Nannine had reached the first pirogue, and Fargo

slowed, folded his long legs into the second craft. He dug the paddle into the water to follow Nannine as she sped away. The rifle exploded a shot far wide of the mark in the darkness, and Fargo kept his head as low as he could as he raced after Nannine, who had her pirogue slicing full speed through the water. He substituted power for skill and still only managed to stay close to her as she raced down the bayou, moving at full speed as she went under the archway and out the other side. She turned into the main bayou, continued to paddle furiously until she reached her cabin. She maneuvered the narrow boat smartly against the dock, moored it by the bow, and was waiting on the warped boards as he paddled to a halt.

"You are hurt," she said, taking in the wound at his side and the marks on his forearm, and she marched him into the cabin. She dug out salve as he lay down on the mattress, rubbed his wounds as he stroked her black tresses.

"I owe you," he said.

"I waited. When you did not come out, I had to go and see," Nannine said.

"That took real courage," Fargo said.

She smiled, almost sheepishly. "Maybe curiosity is greater than fear," she said.

"I'm glad for that," Fargo said, and pulled her face down to his. Her lips joined his at once, opening, wanting, but he pulled away and rose to his feet with her. "Help me find the way back to my horse. It'll be quicker with you along," he said. Nannine nodded, and he followed her outside to see dawn streaking the horizon, the morning mists shrouding the bayous in a white veil.

Nannine moved from the cabin with surefooted steps, and he followed close to her, dogged her heels as she leapt across small patches of swamp, took shortcuts through the tangled mangroves. Suddenly he saw the line of pond cypresses and, beyond, the glistening black and white of the Ovaro beneath the willows.

Nannine clung to him for a long moment as they reached the horse. "Be careful, so you can come back to me again," she murmured.

"I'll try," he told her, and swung onto the horse.

She watched him until he was out of sight beyond the willows.

Fargo pushed the pinto across the fields as the morning sun burned away the last of the mist. It was midmorning when he reached St. Lucifer and pulled up outside the newspaper office.

Joe Alcott rose from behind the desk to meet him, the questions stark in his eyes.

"I found them," Fargo said grimly. "Found the blonde, too."

"The one from the cellar?" Joe frowned.

"The same," Fargo said. "I know now why I didn't see anyone at the roadside, why nobody did." As Joe sank into the chair by the desk, Fargo filled in the details in short, terse sentences, and when he finished, Joe stared at him in openmouthed astonishment.

"Dwarfs. Murdering dwarfs," he said breathlessly. "My God."

"Eldon," Fargo said. "The name Eldon mean anything to you?"

"Yes, the Eldon Insane Asylum. Why?" Joe frowned.

"They had a bowl from there. Maybe you ought to pay a visit and take a look at their old records."

"Can't do that. All their old records were destroyed in a fire some six years back. Sam Hawkins, who ran the place, just up and left soon after, went to Tennessee, I heard," Joe answered.

"Where's that sheriff of yours?" Fargo asked.

"Ray's in the eastern part of the county this week. It'd take two days to find him, another two days before he got back here," Joe answered. "You want to go in after them now, I take it."

"Not into the bayou. They'll be hightailing it out of there now that I got away. Can you put together a posse?" Fargo questioned.

"I can get all the folks nearby who'd had their girls disappear. About ten good men, I'd guess. But it'll take me a day to get everyone all rounded up," Joe said.

"I can't wait. Their trail could be cold by then. I'll go after them now. They'll be heading for Leadville on the Texas border. That's got to be a three-day ride. You meet me there with your men," Fargo said.

"I'll get there as quickly as I can," Joe said, and Fargo nodded and pulled himself onto the Ovaro. He sent the horse into a fast canter out of St. Lucifer, veered right when he reached open land, and cut across the long, flat fields. There was still one unfinished thing he had to do first. Not just settling accounts, he grunted, more important than that. He wanted to be sure there'd be no more unexpected surprises.

When he reached Dark Willows, he rode in hard and skidded the Ovaro to a halt. There was no time left for game-playing.

Gail opened the tall front door as he swung from the pinto. He reached her in three long strides. He met the sympathy in her gray eyes with his own ice-blue eyes, his jaw a hard line.

"I'd hoped to see you. I heard about the two young women in the stanhope," Gail said. "Another terrible thing."

"Wasn't it, though?" Fargo bit out, his eyes boring

into her. He saw the tiny furrow come to her smooth brow as he brushed past her and went into the house.

She closed the door and the furrow in her brow deepened. "What is it?" Gail asked. "Have you come here just to make more accusations?"

"No more accusations, honey, just facts. Your brother here?" he barked.

"Yes." She half-shrugged.

"You sure?" he demanded.

"He's somewhere around." Gail frowned back.

"Somewhere around isn't good enough. I want to know where he is," Fargo said, his ice-blue eyes spearing her.

"Why?" she returned.

"Because it's past time for fancy talk and phony excuses," Fargo flung at her. "I found that rotten little blonde." He saw Gail Bonnard's face go chalk-white, as if the blood had suddenly been drained from her. She swallowed hard as she tried unsuccessfully to regain her composure.

"You found her?" Gail echoed, words coming with difficulty.

"That's right. Got some more news for you. She's behind the disappearances, the killings, all of it," he said tightly. "She, that hulk of hers, and four murdering dwarfs. Or maybe you knew that all the time. Maybe that's not really news to you," he speared harshly.

He saw shock and horror fill the gray eyes and found himself frowning as she spoke to him.

"I didn't know. My, God, I didn't know," she muttered.

"Hell you didn't," he exploded. "You knew who was in your goddamn cellar all the time."

"The kidnappings . . . the killings, I didn't know about that," Gail said.

"What the hell do you know about?" Fargo demanded angrily. He saw her lips open and close as she fought to find words.

"Shut up, Gail," the voice cut in, and he turned to see Tom Bonnard behind him, a big, seven-shot Spencer in his hands, the long rifle barrel aimed directly at his chest. "Move back and drop your gun belt," Tom Bonnard ordered.

"No, Tom. Stop it," Fargo heard Gail say.

"Drop the gun belt, dammit," Tom Bonnard insisted, and raised the big Spencer a notch.

Fargo unbuckled his gun belt and let it slide to the floor. "You hired those bushwhackers," he said to the younger man.

"I told you to back off," Tom Bonnard said defensively.

Gail's voice cut in. "You fool," Fargo heard her hiss at her brother. "You damn fool."

"He wouldn't stop poking and prying. I had no choice," Tom Bonnard shouted back.

"It was wrong, all wrong. It can't go on anymore," Gail said. "Not now, not with what Fargo found out."

"Shut up, Gail, shut up," Tom Bonnard shouted at her, but he didn't take his eyes off the big man in front of him. "Turn around, damn you," he spit at Fargo, his finger nervously twitching alongside the trigger.

Fargo's lips pulled back in distaste as he turned, but the man was near irrationality. He saw Gail's eyes darken with protest as she stared past him at her brother.

"No, Tom, no more," she pleaded.

"That senate seat's just waiting for me and I'm going to get it. The Bonnards are going to keep on running Thurmond county. I'm not letting anything get in my way now," Fargo heard the man snarl. Tom

Bonnard took a step toward him, and Fargo tried to duck away, but the blow landed on the back of his head, the heavy rifle barrel an unyielding club. Fargo went down, Gail's cry of protest a dim and distant sound as he hit the floor.

He tried to fight the blackness that descended over him, but he lost. Yet he clung to enough consciousness to feel himself being pulled, lifted, and dropped. He had a vague awareness of being jarred, and then stillness. Consciousness returned with agonizing slowness, the world coming together in little bits and pieces until finally he could pull his eyes open. He blinked, focused, saw a dim light. Objects began to take shape, steps against the wall, a short stairway leading up, and nearby, a trunk, brass-fitted, an old bedstand. He sat up and cursed. He was in the cellar, the same damn cellar where it had all started.

He got to his feet, shook his head to clear it, strode to the storm door first. It had been locked from outside, and he couldn't find the leverage to break it open from where he stood below. He scanned the dimness and spotted a thick piece of wood beneath the frame of the brass bed. He pulled it out and charged up the steps, held the length of wood in front of him, battering ram fashion, and smashed it into the locked cellar door. He drew back two steps, charged again, and felt the door shake as he crashed the length of wood against it just over the lock. He smashed at the door again, and then again, and each time he saw the door tremble more violently. But it refused to give. He rested a moment, smashed into the door again. He swore, stepped back, raised the length of wood for another charge when he heard the lock being opened.

He stepped to the side, flattened himself against

143

the wall of the stairs, the length of wood upraised as the door opened.

"Fargo," he heard his name called, and saw the long brown hair dip as Gail pushed her head in. He whirled, almost bowled her over as he charged out of the door. He halted as he saw she was alone. The gray eyes were made of pain as she met his angry glance. "I promised I wouldn't let you out," she said.

"Some promises are made to broken," Fargo said, and frowned at her.

"I just don't care anymore," she said, a terrible weariness in her voice. She moved past him into the big living room and sank into a cushioned chair. "It's not what you think. It never was," she said.

"Talk, dammit, and fast," Fargo said. "Start with the damned blonde. You know who she is, dammit."

Gail's gray eyes looked back out of anguish. "Her name's Danela. She's my half-sister," she said softly. "And she's mad, raving mad."

"Tell me something I don't know," Fargo snapped.

"Father had this other woman somewhere, a mistress. None of us ever met her. She was part of his secret life," Gail said.

"Danela's mother," Fargo said.

"Yes, and from the moment Danela was born, he did everything he could to keep her existence a secret. He was determined that there'd be no scandal to hurt the Bonnard name, nothing any of his enemies could use against him."

"From what I've heard, he had plenty of those," Fargo commented.

Gail nodded. "But he succeeded in keeping the girl and her mother a secret. At first, anyway. He used all his power and enough money to buy silence. But Danela's mother died when she was twelve. Father put Danela in with a foster family, inventing a story about her. But it didn't work."

"They found out the truth?" Fargo asked.

"No, but Danela began to do strange and terrible things. She almost killed her foster mother, and they were pretty sure she fixed it so one of the other children was killed. Then she burned the house down. It became plain that Danela was totally mad, insane."

"That's when he sent her to Eldon Asylum," Fargo said, and drew a glance of surprise from Gail.

"Yes, only Danela knew exactly who she was. Her mother had seen to that, and she threatened to tell everything if Father didn't take her out of there," Gail said.

"So he did, and saw to it that all the records were destroyed," Fargo said grimly.

"He had to bring her here to Dark Willows, and he told Tom and myself everything. But he didn't know just how insane she really was. Like many deranged people, she was insanely clever. She had birth records, the name of the midwife, statements by her mother, all kinds of proof hidden away someplace. She threatened Father with it if she didn't get her way. The idea of the scandal was more than he could take. I'm convinced it caused the heart attack that killed him," Gail told him.

"That left Tom to deal with her. Only Tom couldn't stand the idea of scandal any more than your father could," Fargo filled in.

Once again Gail nodded bitterly. "But Danela was getting more and more mad. She hated Tom and hated me even more. She demanded all kinds of things and claimed the house was half hers. That's when Tom worked out the arrangement with her. He agreed to let her use the house by night when we went to New Orleans."

"Now I see why you closed the place up completely and gave the servents the time off," Fargo said.

"Yes, but that's all we knew. Danela used the house by night. We knew nothing else. Neither Tom nor I had any idea that she was behind the girls' being taken, the killings, all of it. We never knew, not until you came here this morning and told me."

"You sure as hell knew about the kidnappings. Everybody in the county did. You never suspected?" Fargo pressed.

"No, I swear it," Gail said almost tearfully.

"You mean you didn't want to know. You didn't want to think about it. You were content to let a girl you knew was murderously insane go free and do whatever she wanted—using your house to do it in—all to avoid a scandal on the family name," Fargo threw back at her. "In my book that makes you both guilty as hell for everything that's happened."

He saw the tears fill the gray eyes. "I see that now," Gail murmured. "I see it now."

"Maybe you do, but not Tom," Fargo snapped.

"He's too much like Father, too ambitious, too much in love with all the Bonnard power and wealth," she said.

"Where is he?" Fargo asked.

"Gone off to hire more men and go into the bayous to find her. He thinks if he can get rid of her once and for all, it'll end her threat to him," she answered.

"He won't find her. She's gone off someplace else," Fargo grunted, spotted his gun belt on a small table, and strode to scoop it up and buckle it on.

"Where are you going?" Gail asked.

"To try to save two girls and put an end to a mad woman and her mad friends," Fargo said.

"I'll go with you," Gail said.

"Why?" He frowned.

"To help. I can ride. I'm a good shot. You can't do it all alone," she said.

"Conscience?" he slid at her, and saw her eyes darken.

"I guess that's part of it," she answered.

"It's all of it, honey. You figure by helping stop her you can wipe away the guilt. No dice. That's too easy a way out for you," he snapped, and strode from the house.

She followed him outside, anger in the gray eyes now. "You're being a bastard," she tossed at him.

"When your brother gets home, you can tell him the party's over," Fargo said, and whirled the Ovaro into a tight circle and struck out across the flat green fields. She had gone inside when he cast a glance back, and he concentrated on making time.

He headed for the place where the blonde and her insane troupe had gone into the bayous with the two girls. They'd have come out at the same place. When he reached it, the sun was already slipping across the afternoon sky. He dismounted, saw the marks where they had emerged from the willows and headed southwest. Three horses, he muttered darkly—riding hard, he noted as he followed. One rode heavily, carring the hulk and Danela, no doubt. The second horse carried the two girls, and the third with the lightest hoofmarks would be carrying the two remaining bloodthirsty dwarfs. Fargo followed and saw they slowed the pace soon enough. He reined to a halt as he came to a tumbledown shack. He dismounted again and scanned the ground. They had picked up a wagon here, he saw, the wagon-wheel marks rolling from inside the empty shack.

He swung back into the saddle and put together the rest of it as he rode on. It was a closed wagon, he was damn sure, but no rockaway or fancy brougham. The wheel treads indicated a delivery or ice wagon. They would have closed sides, too. The girls and the dwarfs were probably inside the wagon, Danela and Igor on the horses. The wagon would slow them down some, and he was grateful for that. They no doubt thought they'd gotten away free, and that would help too.

Night came quickly, and he found a small glen of bitternut and he sank down, tiredness sweeping over him. He set out his bedroll and lay atop it, the night warm and still, and he slept soundly. He guessed he'd been asleep perhaps an hour or two when he snapped awake. He lay motionless for a moment, the hair on the back of his neck tingling. He listened, caught the faint sound again, the soft step of a horse moving along the edge of the bitternut. He rose, the big Colt in his hand, and crept forward. He saw the horse moving slowly, the rider leaning forward in the saddle, trying to pick up hoofprints in the pale light of a new moon. He saw the dark-brown hair hanging forward, almost covering her face, as Gail bent low in the saddle. He let her half-pass the glen when he stepped forward.

"It's no good trying to read a trail by night," he said, saw her head come up, the long brown hair flying to one side as she turned and halted. "Now you can turn around and go back," he growled. He admitted surprise that she had trailed him this far, but he'd concentrated on following his own trail and had let his customary caution lapse.

"No, I'm not going back," Gail said as she slid from the dark-sable standardbred. "I'm going after her with you, and you've no right to stop me." She paused, searched his hard stare. "I know it won't wipe out the past. I'm not taking it as an easy way to salve my conscience. But it'll be something to help make up, and you've no right to deny me that, no right."

He let his lips purse as her words, filled with pain and anger, stabbed at him. "Maybe not," he agreed. "Trying counts." He turned and walked into the glen. "Hitch your horse and get some sleep. I'm going to ride hard tomorrow," he said, and returned to his bedroll. She went into the brush to take off her things, and he smiled.

"Modesty, after that afternoon at the lake?" he called out to her.

"That was different," she returned.

"So it was," he agreed, and understood.

She returned in a light cotton nightgown that fell almost straight from the tips of her full, deep breasts. He turned on his side as she settled down. He was almost asleep when he heard her voice.

"Thank you, Fargo," she said.

"You might want to take that back before this is done with," he murmured, closed his eyes, and let sleep come to him again.

7

She was dressing in the bushes when he woke, and he found a stream to wash in and a stand of blueberries and pears that made a fine breakfast. He picked up the wagon trail quickly and set a steady pace, slowing the horses as the sun grew burning hot and the land began to lose its lushness. Rock gulleys and hillsides grew more plentiful and the soil became dry as the land began to slide toward the Texas border. He followed the trail down through a narrow passage of rocky soil, slowed, and halted to rest at the other end as the sun scorched the earth.

Gail had ridden with him mostly in silence, consumed with her own thoughts, but as he rested beside a trickling stream, she leaned back, her full breasts pushed hard against the lime shirt, her eyes studying him.

"I'm glad you came to find the answers you did," she said. "I'm glad no matter how it turns out."

"It'll mean the truth out in the open," he told her.

"I don't care anymore. It should've been told long ago," Gail said, and he caught something unfinished in her voice and in the way her eyes stayed on him.

"What else?" he asked.

"And I should've let you make love to me that day by the lake," she said.

"You get honest all at once, don't you?" He laughed.

"Why not?" Gail shrugged.

"I'll take a rain check," he said. "Now let's ride."

She followed him as he moved back onto the trail, the horses walking under the hot sun as tree cover grew more and more sparse. But as the day neared an end, the land changed character again, and he saw good brush, good downy bromegrass across Gulf prairieland. A line of gray clouds came with the dusk and hung low. As the dark descended, so did a gentle rain. He found a rock outcrop in a stand of hawthorns fronted by the thick downy bromegrass and tethered the horses in the dryness of the outcrop.

He started to set out his bedroll, halted as he saw Gail standing very still, her gray eyes on him. "It's raining, in case you hadn't noticed," she said.

He straightened up. "So it is," he agreed. "And I've a rain check, don't?" He unbuckled his gun belt, tossed it onto the grass, and pulled off his shirt, kicked off boots and trousers. She remained still, watching, until suddenly, with an explosion of haste, she flung off clothes and stood nude before him, her gray eyes smoldering. He watched the soft rain wet the creamy-white breasts, run down a full figure with a rounded little belly, full, rich thighs no longer hidden by pink bloomers, legs that curved nicely into long calves. His eyes moved slowly upward to the modest little black triangle, the slow swell of her little belly just above it, and back up to the deep, cream-white mounds that rose and beckoned. She had a ghostlike, pale beauty in the night.

He stepped forward, cupped his hands under her breasts, and caressed them. She came against him to press their softness into his skin. The rain had covered her with a wetness that inflamed him. It made smoothness into satin, softness into ductile pliancy. She sank down onto the moist, cool grass, pulled him atop her, and he felt the smooth wetness of the insides of her thighs clasp around him. He bent his mouth to the creamy mounds, sucked and pulled, caressed with his tongue, savoring the tiny pink tips and pink circles. He heard her little sounds of delight. The soft rain ran down his back, exciting him, and beneath him, Gail pushed her wet body against his filled, erect maleness.

"Take me, Fargo. Please take me," she murmured against him, opened her moist thighs, and he felt the wet warmth of where she had clasped herself around him.

He drew up, found her waiting portal, and plunged in, the wetness heavier, the viscosity of passion, and Gail cried out from deep inside her, a throaty sound, low and full of urging. "Aaaaah," she cried out, and his flesh against hers slipped and slid with a cool dampness as the rain grew heavier, and he thrust harder into her. "Oh, God, yes," Gail called out, her voice rising in volume but not in pitch, her words low, throaty, rumbling sounds of pleasure. He sucked on one rain-wet, cream-white mound, let it circle inside his mouth, slide half out and back in again. Her hands came up to press against the back of his neck. "More, more," she groaned, and he increased his thrustings, held inside her, and her groaning sounds grew deeper as her hips rose, rotated, her legs holding him tight inside her.

He felt her rolling up and across as she tried to extract every last drop of sensation from the ecstasy that held her. Suddenly he saw her head fall back, her lips open, and tiny, low gasping sounds came from her. "Now, now, Fargo, now," she grunted, and he felt her hips rotating feverishly, her legs clamped tight around him. Her scream of climax was a roar from someplace deep inside her, tigerish in its tone, absolute in its intensity.

He finally lay atop her as her heaving belly grew still and her legs fell away from his hips. The rain-drops cooled his skin, washed down the exhaustion of passion with gentle moistness, and he stayed with her until she finally moved from under him and sat up on one elbow. She blew a raindrop from the end of her aristocratic nose. "I knew you'd be special from the moment I saw you," she said.

"Best damn rain check I ever had," he said.

She lay back, one leg up, ghostly loveliness in the dark, and he watched the gentle rain trickle across her breasts. "Makes you feel refreshed quickly," she murmured.

"It does," he agreed, half-turned, and found one full breast with his lips. The flesh echoed words, and he felt himself rising at once, nature's lubricant working magic, and Gail's thighs fell open in wel-come instantly. The rain remained gentle, the night still, and passions strong. Once more her deep, rum-bling groan drifted into the night. She came to sleep tight against him afterward, and he felt the rain slowly coming to a stop as he fell asleep.

Morning brought the drying sun, and he had to stir her into wakefulness. He dressed, watched her as she pulled on clothes, her full breasts as lovely in the bright sun as they had been in the wet rain the night before. He hated to see the lime blouse swallow them into modesty.

They had a hard day of riding ahead, and he set a fast pace in the morning and slowed as the sun burned high. Soon the land grew into part marsh and part plains. "We'll make Leadville before the day's done," he told her, and saw her face grow solemn.

153

"Why Leadville? You never told me," she said.

"They're meeting buyers from Mexico there," he answered. "The hulk and those dwarfs, got any idea where she picked up that crew?"

"Maybe from the asylum." Gail shrugged. "She's clever enough to have found a way to get them out."

"Figures. Crazies find other crazies," Fargo said as he glanced skyward and saw the sun slipping over a high hill in the west. He increased the pace, the land growing thick with scraggly brush, hawthorn, and box elder. They had crested a hill when he spotted the roadway. He cantered down to it and followed its curving path. Dusk had begun to touch the land when he turned a bend and saw the town in front of him. A road sign staked into the ground bore the crudely lettered name: LEADVILLE. Fargo slowed the Ovaro and pulled under the wide, low branches of a box elder.

"We wait here till dark," he said. "I don't want them spotting either of us."

"You sure they are here?" Gail questioned.

"I aim to find that out tonight," Fargo said. "I'd guess they are."

"What, then?" Gail asked.

"If they're waiting for the Mexican buyers, we wait too," Fargo told her. "Joe Alcott's on his way to meet me here with a posse."

"And if the Mexicans are here and ready to leave with the girls?" Gail pressed.

"I stop them," Fargo said grimly.

"No," Gail said, and he threw a glance at her. "We stop them," she corrected.

"Fine with me." He shrugged. "You want to work in the kitchen, you've got to take the heat." He settled down against the tree trunk, and Gail sat beside him in silence until night came over the countryside. He checked out the Colt, put a few drops of oil on the gun, and swung onto the pinto, his glance on Gail as she mounted her horse. "Don't get in the way," he warned.

"I won't," she said.

She rode in silence beside him as he headed the half-mile to the town. He turned the Ovaro away from the wide, single street that formed the backbone of the dusty, typical little border town, and rode slowly behind the buildings. He paused between each building to peer out to the street. He saw heavy dead-axle drays, flatbed rigs and a Conestoga, a half-dozen buckboards, and two big Owensboro Texas cotton-bed wagons, but no closed delivery wagons. He swung between two buildings, Gail close behind him, paused at the dance hall, and halted before a figure lounging against a post.

"Got a hotel here?" he asked.

"Hawley's, other end of town," the man said, and Fargo pulled out onto the main street and slowly moved toward the far end of the town.

The hotel marked itself with a wooden sign. It was a two-story frame building that rose almost alongside a second saloon, smaller and dingier than the dance hall in the center of town. Fargo saw a half-drunken figure nursing a bottle seated alongside the side of the hotel, and he dismounted, telling Gail to stay on her horse with a flick of his eyes. The drunk looked up as he approached, his reddened face carrying the perpetual alcoholic's flush, but his eyes surprisingly sharp.

"You see a big, bald-headed giant of a man around here?" Fargo asked.

The drunk shook his head as he took a drain of the bottle in his hand. "Nope. Only been here an hour," the man said, his speech slurred, but his eyes staying sharp. "I could watch for you," he offered. "I'll be here till I finish this bottle. Cost you another bottle."

"I'll think about it," Fargo said, and moved past the man through the narrow space between the hotel and the saloon. He reached the end, peered out, and drew back at once. A light delivery wagon, panels tightly closed, horse hitched to it, rested just behind the hotel. He edged forward again, just enough to let him peer around the side of the wall at the wagon. It was locked tight and closed in completely. The two girls could be bound and gagged inside, and the two dwarfs could be in with them, he realized, keeping guard inside. The chances were too good, and he decided not to go near the wagon as he backed down the alleyway.

He came out in front, and the drunk looked up at him, grayish hair half-falling over the flushed face. "Want me to watch for you?" the man offered hopefully again.

"Still thinking about it. I'll let you know," Fargo said as he climbed onto the pinto, and the drunk waved good-bye with his bottle. Fargo moved past the hotel, aware that Gail had caught the tenseness in his face.

"You found them," she murmured.

"Found the right kind of wagon, only one like it in town," he said. He wound his way into the trees at the edge of town and doubled back in a circle that brought him to the edge of a hawthorn at the rear of the hotel and the silent, closed wagon. He drew the big Sharps from its saddle holster and handed the rifle to Gail.

"I've got to go into the hotel and make sure," he said. "You stay here and watch that wagon. The girls may be inside it."

She nodded as she dismounted with the rifle.

"Anybody tries to take off with it, I shoot," she said, and he nodded.

"Giants, dwarfs, Mexicans, or blondes," he bit out.

She met the question in his eyes. "You can count on it," she said firmly.

"No matter what else happens, you just watch that wagon," he told her. He backed the pinto, made off through the trees, and emerged in front of the hotel. He left the pinto at the hitching post and scanned the windows of the frame structure. They faced front and on both sides. He peered around one corner. The drunk was still seated against the building, nursing his bottle, and Fargo stepped into the hotel. A thin-faced man rose from behind a low counter with a register book on it.

"I'm looking for a blond girl, small, pretty face, hair maybe a little stringy," he said. "Maybe a bald-headed giant with her."

"People come and go. I don't take notice," the man said with surliness.

"You couldn't miss these two," Fargo insisted.

"Folks come in here, they expect privacy," the clerk snapped.

Fargo leaned forward, closed one big hand around the man's shirtfront. "These folks don't deserve privacy, and I expect answers," he growled.

The man swallowed hard as he saw the steel in the big man's lake-blue eyes. "That monster finds out I talked, he'll break me in half," he said.

"You don't talk, and I'll do it now," Fargo said.

The clerk blanched. "The giant came in with her, but he left," the man said.

"Where's the blonde?" Forgo asked.

"Room Six, second floor, right-hand hall," the man said.

Fargo released his shirt as he straightened up.

157

"You did right, cousin. Feel good about it," he said as the clerk sat down, his face ashen. Fargo saw the stairway and took the steps slowly, noiselessly. On the second floor, two hallways branched out, one into the left side of the building, the other the right. Fargo moved down the right-side one and halted at the door marked with a peeling number six. A flickering light edged out through the bottom of the door, and he carefully enclosed the door knob in one huge hand. He turned his fist and felt the door knob move, inched it further, continued to open the door with noiseless caution. When he felt it give, he halted, shifted his feet, and with a lightning-fast spin he sprang into the room and slammed the door shut behind him.

He saw her at once, sitting cross-legged atop the plain bed. A candle flickered from a small table beside her, and she wore the same floor-length loose shift. Her burning blue eyes stared at him, but showed neither surprise nor concern, and the air hung with silence as she neither moved nor spoke.

"It's over," Fargo said finally. Her eyes continued to burn with the strange, inner blue fire that seemed to spear through him as she stared silently back. "The girls in the wagon outside?" he asked.

The edge of a tiny smile touched her lips, and she lifted her arms, pulled the garment over her head, and sat naked before him, slender legs still crossed, her very red nipples pushing forward on the smallish breasts. As he watched, she leaned back, uncrossed her legs by lifting them high, showing him all of her dark, tangled portal, and then swung lightly from the bed. She began to sway, her small, naked body undulating sinuously as a tiny whistling sound escaped her lips. She swayed, half-turned, moved her hips back and forth as she slid across the floor on bare feet. Her smallish breasts jiggled as she shook her body, halted, shimmied again, and slid silently across the floor. Her burning eyes continued to blaze with their strange light.

Fargo watched her in fascination as she slowly turned to the left, then right, shimmied again, and undulated to the little whistling sound from her lips. He had dared her to dance for him back in the bayou, and now she was taking his dare as if nothing had happened before or since.

She lifted her arms as he watched, the frown digging into his brow, spun slowly, and suddenly, with explosive speed, smashed one extended arm against the candle and plunged the room into darkness. He heard her furious hiss, not unlike that of a cougar's snarl. He saw the dark blur come at him. He twisted away, but she leapt atop him, and he felt her nails clawing at his neck, trying to reach his face. He dropped, swung his body, and flung her from his back. The room seemed filled with her wild hissing snarls now, and he drew the Colt, staying on one knee as he tried to peer through the blackness of the room. The burning blue eyes could apparently see in the dark like a cat, and he heard her coming at him again. Too late, he saw the top of the bedstand table as the edge of it crashed into his forehead with a burst of pain. He went down and the leg of the table landed on his wrist and the Colt dropped out of his hand.

He twisted as he saw her form leaping over the upended table at him. She landed on his back again, raked down with her nails, and tried to reach around to his throat. "Goddamn crazy bitch," Fargo roared in fury as he flung himself up. She lost her grip and slid down his legs. He pulled away, kicked out, felt his foot smash into flesh, and heard her snarled gasp.

He backed through the blackness, which was again filled with the wild hissing snarls, heard her bare feet dart back and forth across the room.

She was at the dresser in a corner of the room, and he heard her yank a drawer open. He turned, glimpsed the thin edge of moonlight from behind the curtain at the window, and dived. He yanked at the curtain with both hands and ripped it down. The moonlight flooded into the room through the window, pale and wan, but he welcomed it as he would a bonfire. He saw her naked body rushing at him, crouched, about to spring, and he caught the gleam of the long-bladed kitchen knife in her hand.

He tried to spot the Colt on the floor, but quickly gave up the idea and stayed in a crouch as he saw her come at him. She had the maniacal strength and the speed to cut his head off, he realized, and he stayed motionless, watching her near. The blue eyes burned, but her round face had become composed. Her smallish breasts swayed in unison and her blond hair fell attractively around her face. He frowned in awe. She somehow managed to look pretty. She was trying to kill him, and she was pretty and insane and almost unbelievable. He watched her take a step closer, the knife upraised in one hand. She'd leap with the speed of a cougar and the strength of ten men, he knew, and his eyes were riveted on her. He felt the message go through his muscles as he caught the faint dip of her knees, held a split second longer, and was ready as she hurled herself through the air, her pretty mouth breaking into a hissing snarl.

He reached one long arm up, caught the wrist with the knife, flung himself backward with her, and catapulted her over his head. She flew higher and farther than he'd thought she would. Her naked body sailed over his head, and he heard the sharp, shattering sound of the window smashing into a thousand pieces as she went through it. There was no scream from her, only a long hiss, and he leapt to his feet, ran to the smashed window, and peered down. Her naked body lay on its back, her head twisted brokenly to one side. She had landed less than a half-dozen feet from the drunk still holding his bottle, and he stared at her in openmouthed astonishment.

Fargo turned from the window, took the steps down the stairs three at a time, and raced outside and around to the side of the hotel.

Danela Bonnard hadn't moved. She would never move again. She looked so slender and young and pretty. Only her eyes had changed. They no longer burned with blue fire. The drunk had staggered to his feet and stared down at her, then liffed his eyes to Fargo, a frown of consternation on his flushed face. "Jeez, mister, she was good for another fifteen years at least," he muttered.

"I've always been wasteful." Fargo shrugged and strode away.

He moved to the end of the alleyway and peered out. The closed wagon was still there, silent as a tomb on wheels, and somewhere under the big hawthorn, Gail watched and waited. She had to have heard the shattering crash of the window, and she undoubtedly wondered what it meant. She'd have to keep wondering, he muttered silently as he moved back through the alleyway. A small crowd had come out of the saloon to stare down at the blond, naked figure, and he edged his way around them.

"Somebody get Buryin' Joe Getch," he heard a voice call out, and two of the figures began to walk up the street. Fargo started toward the Ovaro when the huge shape materialized out of the darkness. He stayed back as Igor strode to where the small knot of figures still gathered together, and Fargo watched him push his way through the onlookers. He saw the giant halt, stare at the ground for a long moment, and suddenly raise his bald-head upward to the sky. A tremendous, bellowing roar came from the huge throat, a sound to make a grizzly tremble.

Just as suddenly, the giant whirled, his tree-trunk arms striking out, and two of the onlookers were sent sprawling a dozen feet. Another roar of rage came from the huge man as he seized a figure, lifted the unlucky onlooker into the air, and flung him into the side of the hotel. The others tried to flee, but the giant caught one man and smashed him to the ground with one hammerlike blow. Two other figures tried to flee, collided with each other, and the giant was on them instantly.

"Over here, you stinkin', murderin' monster," Fargo shouted as he stepped forward. The giant halted. When he saw Fargo, he dropped his hold on the two men and came toward him. As Fargo watched, the bald head seemed to grow red, the giant's face contorted, and a bellow of rage erupted from the huge neck, where veins stood out as though they were muscles. The giant charged at him with the fury of a wounded buffalo, and Fargo flung himself sideways at the last moment as the hulk swept past him. He knew all too well the strength of the man, and now the giant was enraged to insensate fury.

Fargo pushed his foot out as the huge form went past him, and the giant sprawled headlong on the ground. The monstrous figure turned to rise, and Fargo's boot caught him flush on the point of the jaw. The crack of bone sounded almost like a shot.

The giant fell back, rose, his jaw hanging limply to one side as he charged again, a stream of blood running from his mouth. Fargo waited, ducked away from two sweeping blows of the treelike arms. As the giant spun around, Fargo crashed a looping left hook onto the broken jaw. Igor bellowed as much with rage as with pain, lashed out with a backward swipe that Fargo managed only to partly duck, and the blow sent him sprawling. He rolled, avoiding a crushing stomp as the giant leapt forward with both feet and landed hard.

Fargo hit him in the stomach with an arching right that would have torn the insides loose from most men. The giant didn't even double up and quickly smashed another backhanded blow that Fargo took across the back of his shoulders. It sent him sprawling. But he recovered quickly as he heard the tremendous footsteps crash down again only inches from his head.

He rose, ducked another lunge, and crashed a right to the hanging jaw once more. The huge figure only came at him again, his lower face a swollen, shapeless mass. Fargo threw another hard right into the giant's stomach and fell backward to avoid a sweeping blow. Igor's little eyes were red, and Fargo smelled an acrid odor from the huge form. The brute was nothing but insensate rage, incapable of feeling even extraordinary pain. He was beyond all the human senses.

Fargo backtracked, reached down, and drew the thin, razor-sharp, double-edged throwing knife from its holster around his calf. He backed again and measured. As the hulk lunged at him, Fargo flung the knife with all his strength. The blade buried itself into the huge form's midsection. The giant halted, reached one monstrous hand up, yanked the knife out of his flesh, and threw it aside. He charged forward again, and Fargo sidestepped the lunge. He wasted no time in trying to strike back as he dived for the knife on the ground, scooped it up, and whirled to face the charging figure again.

The monster raced at him, arms outstretched, blood pouring from the front of his stomach without effect on him. Fargo backed again, lifted the slender blade, took another few steps back to give himself time to aim. He let Igor gather speed once more, roar in at him as he flung the knife. This time the long, narrow blade embedded itself into the giant's throat just over the collarbone. The monstrous form slowed, staggered, and once again reached a hand up and pulled the blade free. But the red that gushed from his throat was a torrent. He swayed, put both huge hands to his neck, but the torrent of red only flowed around the thick fingers.

The giant swayed, dropped to his knees, swayed again, and pitched forward onto his face. The big bald head began to stain with red as it lay in the widening pool of blood.

Fargo drew a deep breath, walked to the mountainous figure, and bent down. He pushed the lifeless form half over on its side to retrieve the thin blade. He walked past the shocked, staring eyes of the clerk outside the entrance to the hotel, and went upstairs to Room Six, where he finally found the Colt under the bed.

The crowd had grown larger and louder when he returned downstairs, and he avoided the gathering and went down the alleyway again. The closed wagon was still there, still waiting and silent, and Fargo swore under his breath. He backed away, went around the crowd again that stared at the huge, lifeless figure, and climbed onto the pinto.

He circled back through the trees and edged the horse under the big hawthorn where Gail waited, her eyes flooding with relief as she spotted him. "My

God, you're alive," she said breathlessly, and clung to him when he slid to the ground. "I almost left, almost came looking," she said.

"I'm glad you didn't. I still think the girls are in that wagon," Fargo said.

"What happened? It was terrible hearing the noise and not knowing anything," Gail said.

"She's dead. The hulk, too," Fargo said.

Gail leaned against the tree. "I can't feel anything but relief," she said, and saw his eyes fastened on the wagon. "Maybe there's nobody in there," she said. "Maybe they made the trade already, and the girls are on their way to Mexico and the wagon's just sitting there."

Fargo grimaced at the possible truth in her words, but one thing jabbed at him. "Where are those two stinking, murdering dwarfs?" he asked.

"Gone off on their own someplace?" Gail ventured.

"Not likely. Danela was still here; the hulk, too. They were a team, all dependent on one another. They'd stay together even if the deal had been made. I say they're in that wagon," Fargo thought aloud. He stared at the wagon and his eyes narrowed in thought. The delivery wagon had double doors in the rear and a lighter single door that closed the front section off from the driver's seat. He let his gaze measure distances along the ground as the plan took shape in his mind.

"Give me three minutes," he said to Gail. "Then you move out and slowly ride toward the wagon from the rear. Flatten yourself low in the saddle and move slow."

"They'll see me, of course, if they're in there," Gail said.

"That's right. They'll see you and you'll have all

their attention. They'll be wondering about you for a few moments at least, wondering and watching. I'll just need a few seconds," Fargo said, and Gail nodded.

He left the Ovaro under the tree and moved forward in a crouch, circled through the trees until he was opposite the front of the wagon. The horse hitched to it stayed quietly half-asleep, he noted as he crawled to the edge of the trees. He counted off minutes and saw Gail emerge from the trees at the rear of the wagon. She walked the horse forward slowly and stayed flattened over its neck, he saw in satisfaction. He waited and watched.

She halted, then slowly moved forward again. He smiled grimly. She was doing a good job. Their attention would be riveted on her. He let a dozen more seconds go by, and as she halted again, he bolted from the trees and raced forward with his long, powerful legs. He swept past the horse, vaulted onto the wagon in one bound, dug his heels into the driver's seat for added momentum and smashed headlong into the door.

It crashed open, and he saw the two girls on the floor to one side of the wagon and the two misshapen, stunted forms whirl in surprise from the little window at the rear door. One yanked a knife from his waist, but Fargo kicked out and the thick-bodied little form flew backward. The second one dived low, came at his legs, and he saw the short-handled ice pick in the dwarf's hands. He flung himself sideways as the dwarf lashed out with a vicious swipe. He missed and the pick embedded itself in the side of the wagon.

Fargo drew his Colt, slammed the heavy barrel down onto the dwarf's head as he struggled to pull the pick free. He saw the little figure sink down out of the corner of his eye as he whirled to see the other one, the knife thrust forward, leaping toward the two girls on the floor of the wagon. Fargo fired, and the sides of the light delivery wagon shook with the sound of the shot. The short, squat figure seemed to do a back flip as it slammed into a corner of the wagon, stayed there for a second, then crumpled lifelessly to the floor.

Fargo heard a sound at his side, spun to see that the last crazed little man had shaken off the blow, pulled the pick free, and was rushing at him with the weapon sweeping up in a deadly arc. Fargo flung himself backward, and the needle-sharp ice pick grazed his groin. The little squat figure spun with monkeylike agility and lunged forward again. But this time Fargo had the Colt ready. Once again the wagon shook with the sound of the shot, and the dwarf flew backward as if he'd been catapulted. He landed at the feet of the crumpled form in the far corner of the wagon, another small, misshapen, lifeless mound.

Fargo stepped forward, kicked the rear doors of the wagon open, and saw Gail there, the rifle in hand, her gray eyes round with fear. He reached down, lifted the two girls to their feet and out of the wagon. Their wrists were bound to each other, and he severed the ropes as Gail herded them from the wagon. Fargo's glance flicked to the two still little mounds inside the wagon. The mad came in all shapes and sizes, the big and the little and the deceivingly pretty, he reflected. "Just like the rest of us," he muttered aloud as he turned away and followed Gail and the two girls into the trees.

He put May Hobson and Valerie on Gail's horse, and Gail shared the Ovaro with him as they rode from town. They found a place to camp at the edge of the road. He rode back into Leadville, rustled up some food at the dance hall, and brought it back. Added a bottle of bourbon, too. When he returned, the two girls were slowly beginning to shake away their fear and despair.

"Joe and the posse ought to be riding in tomorrow," Fargo said. "We'll stay here and wait."

"Sort of a wasted trip for them," Gail said.

"Guess again," Fargo said, and she frowned. "There are two Mexican buyers due anytime. They'll know what's happened to the other girls that were taken. Maybe we can get them all back."

"Is there a chance?" Gail asked.

"There's always a chance," Fargo said. "Now let's get some sleep." He stretched out, and Gail lay close against him as he let exhaustion sweep away all else until he woke with the morning sun. May and Valerie were still asleep, and he didn't wake them; their young faces were still white and drained.

"You stay here with them," he told Gail. "Joe and the others will likely be coming down the road. They arrive before I get back, you hold them here."

She nodded, and he took the Ovaro slowly back into Leadville. The town was awake, the dance hall open day and night, and he tethered the horse to the hitching post and sat down on a barrel a few yards from the dance-hall doors. He watched those who rode through town. Plenty of drifters passed by, the kind every border town attracted, and a sizable number of homesteaders in ramshackle wagons, as well as a handful of prospectors with their pack mules. The morning had almost passed when he saw the two men riding slowly down the street, and his eyes narrowed. The two riders halted in front of the dance hall and dismounted. Mexicans, he grunted silently, from their flat, wide-brimmed *poblanos* and Spanish

saddle rig adorned with silver *conchas* to their ornamented boots and fringed *tapaderos*.

He slid from the barrel and followed the two Mexicans into the dance hall, where they sat down at a
table, their black eyes moving across the few customers seated and the handful of men at the bar. They
settled back, plainly waiting for someone, and
ordered tequila from the girl that came to the table.

Fargo let them wait, almost finish their drinks
before he drifted over to them. Both men glanced up
as he approached. Both had sharp-nosed faces, thin
mustaches, and eyes that glinted with suspicion.

"You wait for the *señorita*?" Fargo asked.

One of the Mexicans with a silver ring hooked into
a leather string tie around his neck shrugged.
"Maybe," he said as he surveyed the big man with
the lake-blue eyes.

"You expected the big one," Fargo slid out.

"Maybe," the man said, and Fargo smiled to himself. They knew who he meant. They were the right
pair.

"Yes or no?" Fargo said, holding to the role.

"Maybe," the Mexican answered.

"He won't be here," Fargo said, and saw the faint
flicker inside the man's eyes. "Neither will she." The
two men peered at him with their eyes suddenly
narrowed.

"Who are you?" the one asked.

"I have the girls," he said, and the Mexicans didn't
change their expressions but held him in a long stare.
"We can't talk here," Fargo said, turned, and walked
to the door. He glanced back to see the two men following. He walked between two buildings and back
from the main street until he found a quiet place. He
halted and waited, and the two men appeared, wary
interest in their faces now.

"Who are you? Where is the señorita?" the one asked.

"Her deal's off. I've got a better one," Fargo said.

The two men eyed him with stolid stares. "You are talking, hombre. Go on," the one said. "What is this deal of yours?"

"Simple. You tell me where the rest of the girls are or I kill you," Fargo said, and saw the men's brows lift.

The one with the silver ring reacted first. He started to draw the gun at his hip. Fargo's hand went to the big Colt, a motion too fast for the eye to follow, and the revolver barked. The bullet drove the silver ring into the Mexican's chest as it struck, and the man staggered backward, fell as if poleaxed. Fargo saw the other one's hand frozen halfway to his holster as he stared down at his partner.

"He have a hearing problem?" Fargo asked blandly. The second Mexican looked up at him, swallowed hard. "Hope you don't have one," Fargo said pleasantly.

"No, señor, no," the man said, fear replacing the suspicion that had been in his eyes.

"I told you my deal," Fargo said, and waited.

"The other girls are at Sánchez's house. We are just couriers. Sánchez buys, trades, runs his house," the man said.

"Where?" Fargo questioned.

"Matamoros," the man said.

"Where's that?"

"In Tamaulipas," the man answered, and Fargo nodded. Tamaulipas state was right over the Texas border from Brownsville on the Gulf.

"Give me your gun," he said, and the man obeyed instantly. Fargo led him back to the horses, took both the Mexican mounts, and forced the man to ride in front of him as he made his way back to the camp where Gail waited with the girls. They'd found company, he saw as he rode up to the eight horses gathered near the trees. He saw Joe detach himself from the other men and hurry to meet him.

"Sorry you had to go it alone. We rode hard as we could," he said, his arm still in the sling, Fargo saw.

"Was afraid to wait," Fargo said, and saw Joe's eyes go to the Mexican. "This gentleman has wisely decided to show us the fastest route to Tamaulipas. The other girls that were taken are there, as many as are still alive," Fargo said.

Joe nodded. "I'll send two of the others back with May and Valerie. Her pa will be one," he said, and Fargo nodded agreement.

"How many will that leave us?" he asked.

"Six, seven with you," Joe said.

"Eight," the voice said, and he turned to see Gail. "I'm going. I want to see it through, all the way," she said.

He started to turn her down when Joe Alcott cut in. "We'll need every gun we can get, and I know she can shoot," Joe said.

Fargo frowned at him, but he saw something unsaid in Joe Alcott's eyes. He pushed the frown from his face and shrugged agreement as he slid from the horse and stretched out on the grass. The others saw to it that the two girls and their escorts were sent on their way.

Fargo rose when Joe came over to him and introduced the men he'd rounded together. They were all older men, none of them sharpshooters, he wagered. But they were steady, and each had a personal stake in getting back all the girls they could find. He'd seen far worse posses, he decided.

"Let's ride," he said, and swung onto the Ovaro.

He rode beside the Mexican as the man swung south to hug the curving line of the Gulf Coast. They rode hard, brought down some Texas jackrabbits for dinner, and Fargo eyed the Mexican. He knew the man would be no problem. He was frightened, aware any attempt at flight would earn him a pine box, but more important, he seemed relieved to be through with his task. He believed the man when the Mexican told him that he'd only followed orders.

Gail came over to him when the meal was ended and sat close.

"You expect anything but hard riding and sound sleeping, you made a mistake, honey," he told her.

"I didn't expect more. But there'll be the trip back," she said.

He nodded and refrained from reminding her that there was no guarantee anyone would be going back. He fixed his bedroll, and she slept at his side, exhausted, and he had to wake her when morning came. She was changing behind tall brush when he called Joe Alcott over.

"Why?" he asked, and Joe knew what it meant at once.

"There's no reason for her to hurry back now," Joe said. "Tom Bonnard came by my place. He hadn't found the blonde, of course, but he realized it would all come out in the open soon. He shot and killed himself the next day."

"Jesus," Fargo murmured.

"He couldn't face it," Joe said. "Funeral's done with by now. Relatives took care of things. It'll be all picking up pieces for her when she gets back. Seeing this through will help her, give her something to hold up with pride."

"Let's ride," Fargo said bitterly.

8

Tamaulipas state was a hot, dusty, and dry place. The trip had been made of backbreaking riding, and Fargo called a halt when the group crossed the border into Mexico. The town of Matamoros was only another few hours on.

"We sleep, get in as much as we can, make up for the past week," he ordered as he camped under a cluster of short blackjack oaks. They stayed the day and night, and when the next morning came, he felt refreshed for the first time since they'd begun. The others felt the same, he was certain, proof in their faces that showed the lines of exhaustion dimmed if not wiped away.

Only the Mexican had grown more nervous. "I am a dead man, señor," he muttered. "Unless you kill Sánchez."

"You can figure there's a damn good chance of that. Tell me about him and his place," Fargo said.

"Sánchez is a fat man with a small head and maybe ten very bad *bandoleros* as guards," the man said. "His place is the biggest house in Matamoros, all white. Vaqueros come from all over Tamaulipas to spend a night with his girls. But the *gringo* girls he keeps downstairs for very special customers who can pay *mucho dinero*."

"You can't just walk in and ask for them," Fargo said.

"No, and he would get suspicious if you all came in and wanted gringo girls. It is the wealthy Mexican landowners who want the yanqui girls. Americans who go to Sánchez want Mexican girls."

"Figures," Fargo grunted. He glanced up to see Joe and the others had gathered around, Gail at one end. "Which means I've got to get downstairs while the rest of you be ready upstairs," he said. He turned to the Mexican. "Is there a separate way downstairs?"

"In the back. That's where he brings in the girls and the special customers for them," the man said.

"Good. That's where I'm going to bring him in a new girl," Fargo said, and his eyes went to Gail. She blinked and then nodded. "Rough yourself up some, pull your shirttails out, cut a tear in your skirt," he said, and gathered the others around him as she left. He gave orders in quick, terse sentences, and when he finished, he drew grave nods of understanding.

"Sánchez has his bandoleros standing around mostly upstairs. No fair draw when the shooting starts. We'll be outgunned. Speed and surprise are our only advantage. Gun them down as fast as you can. Think about your daughters and nieces. That'll help you blast them away."

"We'll give you fifteen minutes," Joe said as Fargo rose.

"Don't forget, you go in asking for Mexican girls," Fargo reminded the men as he turned to see Gail coming toward him. She had messed her hair, let her shirt hang out, only two buttons closed, her deep breasts all but spilling their cream-white mounds out.

"Very good," he said, and wrapped her wrists in a length of lariat. He led her out of the camp, the rope going back to her bound wrists as she sat the dark sable and practiced glowering. He glanced back at her as they entered Matamoros, the town made up of the usual flat-roofed, stucco Mexican buildings with a few stone adobelike houses mixed in.

"I'm just wondering what I ought to ask for you. I don't want to overprice the merchandise," he said.

"Bastard," she hissed, and her glower grew real. He laughed, but grew solemn as he drew up before a large white house with a stone fence around a wide, arched entranceway. A dozen horses were tethered in the courtyard, and he saw two of the *bandoleros* eye him as he entered. He steered the Ovaro toward the back of the house with Gail in tow. One stepped forward at once and raised his hand.

"Tell Sánchez I want to see him in the back," Fargo said.

"You stay here," the man ordered, and disappeared inside the house. He returned in moments, a figure following him. The Mexican's description of Sánchez has been entirely accurate, Fargo noted. Except for the mean slash of a mouth in the jowled face and the shrewd little eyes that took him in at once, flicked to the girl on the horse behind him.

"I want to talk," Fargo said.

"Go ahead," Sánchez answered.

"Not here," Fargo said, and moved the Ovaro on to the back of the house. Sánchez followed quickly, and Fargo saw the wide doorway that led down six stone steps into the house. He gestured to Gail. "She's yours, for the right price," Fargo said.

"What makes you think I want *putas gringas*?" Sánchez asked.

"I know," Fargo said. "This one's special." He watched Sánchez take in Gail, linger on the cream-

175

white mounds that pushed up from the open neckline of the blouse.

"Get off the horse," Fargo ordered harshly, and Gail slid to the ground and let one long, lovely leg show as she did. "You haven't got any like this," Fargo said to the man.

Sánchez fastened his shrewd little eyes on him. "Who sent you to Sánchez?" he asked.

"Nobody, but I know you do business with the señorita yanqui. I can get better ones for you, all like this," Fargo said.

Sánchez eyed Gail again, walked slowly around her, and Gail's glower was more than acting, Fargo knew. "I could just take her from you," Sánchez sneered, and Fargo saw four bandoleros suddenly appear with carbines in their hands. He leaned forward in the saddle.

"Not without a bullet in your fat belly," he said. "And a bullet from this gun will go through even your gut." He saw Sánchez spy the big Colt that was pointed at him over the saddle horn.

Sánchez let his small face break into an oily smile. "You have nerve, gringo," he said. "Bring her downstairs."

Fargo swung from the Ovaro and yanked Gail after him. He heard her muttered curse as he followed Sánchez down the steps and into the house. He found himself in a large room, where eight smaller rooms, each with a curtain over the arched doorway, formed a half-moon. His eyes moved across the big room and, against the far wall, he counted seven girls. He tried to match descriptions with faces and gave up. It would take time to make these fearful, haunted-eyed, abject young women fit what they had once been. But they were alive, at least those in front of him. There were some past rescuing, he was certain. Three *bandoleros* were spaced across the room, stony-faced, arms folded across their chests.

Sánchez went over to Gail and unbuttoned the two buttons. He pulled back her blouse, and Fargo noted his little eyes light up at what he saw. Fargo counted back and decided that Joe and the others had had time to arrive and go upstairs. "How much?" he heard Sánchez ask.

Fargo dropped the rope holding Gail, stepped to her, and untied her wrists. He spun her around, unbuttoned the skirt, and let it hang loose for Sánchez to take in the full, lovely legs. He backed away from Gail, his eyes flicking to the three guards.

"How much, *hombre*?" he heard Sánchez ask again, annoyance in his voice this time. Fargo moved to his left and positioned himself. He wanted to snarl an answer to Sánchez, but he held his tongue. He couldn't afford the luxury of angry answers, the precious seconds that would give the slave trader and his guards time to act.

"What is the matter with you, *gringo*?" he heard Sánchez bark.

"Not a damn thing now," Fargo snarled, and the big Colt seemed to leap into his hand. He fired in an arc, from left to right, slamming shots into the three *bandoleros* first, then pouring three bullets into Sánchez's fat midsection. He saw the man's little eyes widen in horror as he staggered backward and looked down at his protruding belly, which spurted red. The three guards had fallen where they stood and lay on the floor, their guns still holstered.

"Get the girls," Fargo yelled at Gail, and she put her skirt on as she ran across the floor.

Forgo reloaded as Sánchez slowly sank down, hands clasped to his huge stomach. He looked not

177

unlike a pyramid of ice cream that was melting down, his little eyes glazing over.

Fargo heard the explosion of gunfire from the floor upstairs, the fusillade of shots almost deafening. Only the screams of the girls rose over the sound, and he turned and saw Gail pushing the girls toward him. They were running, their haunted eyes filling with hope, their desperation turning into something they never expected to have again. He led the way up the stone steps, saw two more guards racing toward him, rifles in hand, and dropped to one knee, fired, and the men fell, their shots going wild. He raced outside to see Joe riding in with three horses in tow, and he pushed the girls on, two per horse, as Gail swung onto the Ovaro with him.

Another fusillade of shots echoed as he raced the Ovaro alongside the white wall and through the arched gateway. He glanced back, saw the others coming after him.

"We lose anybody?" he called to Joe.

"No. Sam McCarver got hit, leg wound; Tad Downs, too, nothing we can't fix," Joe called back.

Fargo bent low in the saddle, his arms around Gail as she hunched down in front of him. He didn't halt until they had crossed the border and pulled up under a spread of horse chestnuts.

He let the reunions take place first, waited to one side with Gail clinging to him.

"It was terrible, brutal, merciless," she murmured, her eyes still filled with shock.

"It was," he said. "And they deserved all of it, every damn one of them."

Joe came over to him, exhaustion in his face. "We haven't brought back everyone. Didn't expect we would. But it was miracle enough," he said. His eyes met Fargo's level stare. "I'll be taking everyone back now," he said.

"We'll be back a while later," Fargo said, and felt Gail's hand tighten around his arm. She rested her head against him as Joe returned to the others.

"Thanks," she said. "Make me forget everything that's happened, Fargo. I want to think only of you around me, inside me, with me. Make me forget all the yesterdays."

"I'll throw in the tomorrows, too," he said.

The trip back would be a time for pleasure, all the senses indulged. There'd be time enough for remembering. Maybe, when he finally brought her home, he'd even pay another visit to the bayous, he mused. But he knew better. When he brought Gail home he'd head for the prairie winds and the high mountain forests. He'd had too much of swamps and hanging moss. But he'd remember a proud Louisiana beauty caught up in things beyond her and a swamp girl named Nannine. Especially when the Wyoming northerners blew on the long winter nights.

LOOKING FORWARD!
The following is the opening section
from the next novel in the exciting
Trailsman series from Signet:

The Trailsman #50
BLOOD OATH

1861—New Mexico Territory,
where gold-fevered white men
clash with the Apache . . .

The Trailsman swore and flung another shot at the
rocks above him. An answering fusillade caused him
to duck down and simmer in frustration while the
rounds—like angry hornets—ricocheted about his
head and shoulders.

"Shit," he muttered furiously as he swiftly
reloaded his Colt.

Skye Fargo, a large, powerful man all of six feet
tall, with enormous shoulders and an upper torso
alive with muscles that stood out like mole tunnels,
finished reloading his Colt. He peered through his
hawklike eyes at the rocks high above him on the
canyon rim and shook his head in massive frustration. From the very beginning, this foray south of the
border had brought him nothing but trouble. And
now it looked as if the herd of prime horseflesh he
and this scabrous outfit were driving to Tularosa just

might not make it after all. Served him right for trying to do two things at once: make himself rich while chasing after those two gunslicks he had heard about. As it turned out, they hadn't been the men he was searching for, and a less determined man would have been discouraged.

Among the rocks above, an Apache showed his head. Fargo waited. After the Apache's head came his shoulders. A bleak smile on his face, Fargo fired. The Apache went reeling back out of sight, giving Fargo some comfort.

First had come the *bandidos* and now these Children from Hell. They must have traded for Spencer repeaters somewhere, and they were firing down at them with more enthusiasm than skill. Otherwise, not one of Fargo's men would have escaped this ambush. But the Apaches fire had been enough to down two of his men. One was dead, another badly wounded.

Turning about, Fargo peered down the canyon and was relieved to see the rest of his outfit driving the herd out of the canyon, heading north for Tularosa. The dust kicked up by the herd almost obscured them, but it looked as if most of the horses had eluded the Apaches. That was something, at least. Soon, Fargo expected, some of his men would peel back to give him a hand with these damn Apaches. The herd kept moving, and before long the dust had settled back to earth behind them, revealing an empty trail.

Fargo turned back to the Apaches. They occupied the high rocks on the southern rim of the canyon, and their inaccurate fusillade was constant enough to be dangerous. Dirty and dog-tired, the Trailsman lifted his head warily to let his eyes search the rimrocks above. Seeing nothing, he turned, and keeping his tall frame hunched so that it wouldn't be skylined, he moved swiftly down the steep slope to the nearest of his two downed men.

His name was Tom Rifkin. Fargo grabbed his shoulder and rolled him over. The bullet had caught Rifkin in the neck and ranged up into his skull. The skin under his right eye was puffy and black. Over Rifkin's bloody mouth swarmed a cluster of green-bellied flies. Fargo nudged Rifkin back over onto his belly and glanced skyward. The buzzards were already coasting in the hot updrafts high above the canyon floor, like giant cinders from a wood fire. Leaving Rifkin, he continued down the slope to his other wounded partner, Walt Tennyson.

Of all the men he had recruited for this drive, Fargo respected and liked Walt Tennyson the most. Walt had propped himself up against a boulder and was grinning at Fargo through pain-slitted eyes. As Fargo knelt beside him, he started to say something, but instead began to cough weakly, wiping sweat off his pale forehead with the back of his forearm. His hat had tumbled off his head and lay on its crown some distance down the slope. The neat bullet hole in Walt's sweat-darkened checked shirt was just above the fleshy part of his left shoulder.

"How you doing, Walt?" Fargo asked.

"I'll live," he told Fargo. "Where's the horses?"

Fargo gestured with his head. "Down the slope."

The man turned his head to see for himself. Walt's sorrel was standing in the shade of a boulder, its still-heaving sides dripping sweat. Beside it, idly cropping the grass under the boulder, was Fargo's pinto. Fargo wondered if the Apaches' persistence might possibly be related to an eagerness on their part to gain possession of his mount. The Ovaro was a handsome, powerful animal—qualities the Apaches would sure as hell appreciate.

"I can make it that far by myself," Walt said. "Give me a hand, will you?"

Fargo helped the man to his feet, and with Walt's right arm slung around Fargo's shoulder, the two men started down the treacherous, shale-littered slope. They were almost to Walt's horse when a round from almost directly overhead slammed into Walt's back. He went sprawling facedown.

Fargo whirled, caught sight of the Apache outlined against the bright, cloudless sky, and sent two quick shots up at him. The Apache dropped his rifle and toppled from his perch.

Keeping low, Fargo crabbed sideways to examine Walt. The man gasped in panic, "Jesus, Fargo, this time I'm hurt bad!"

Examining him closely, Fargo saw where this second slug had entered high on Walt's shoulder.

"Where's it hurt?" he asked.

"That's just it! I got no feeling in my legs," Walt told him, his eyes bugging wide with astonishment. "I can't move them! My God, Fargo, I'm paralyzed!"

A sudden flurry of more rifle fire sent rounds whining among the rocks all around them. Keeping his head down, he studied the entrance wound on Walt's shoulder. After entering high on Walt's shoulder, the round must have ranged down his back and across the spine, severing it.

Fargo started to drag the big man down the slope toward the horses. His intention was to tie Walt over his saddle; then, leading Walt's sorrel, ride out of the canyon. Just before he reached the sorrel, however, an unseen marksman above him fired three spaced shots, the slugs kicking up dust a dozen yards short of Fargo. A fourth bullet whined past Fargo's head and caromed off a ledge behind him, slamming into Walt's sorrel and catching the animal in the chest. Its forelegs buckled as if they had been cut off at the knees. Threshing its legs feebly as it lay on his side, the sorrel let out one last shrill nicker and died.

"Fargo, I ain't going to make it," Walt gasped weakly.

"Sure, we are," Fargo insisted as he looked back up at the rocks for the Apaches. The bastards had ducked back down, but he caught shadows and saw how close they were getting as they kept inching forward.

Fargo glanced down the canyon. Shit! When were those men of his going to double back to give him a hand?

"Fargo," Walt said, "I got something important to tell you. I want you to listen."

"I'm listening," the Trailsman said, still squinting up at the rocks through the blazing sun. "Go ahead."

"I want you to give my share of this herd to Donna Alvarez in Tularosa."

Fargo glanced in surprise down at Walt. "Donna Alvarez? Who the hell is she?"

"Never mind that. She's the one bankrolled me, gave me the stake to join this damned enterprise. I want her to have my share. Will you see to it?"

Fargo was amazed at the request. Not once during this entire operation had Walt mentioned this woman's name. "You sure about this, Walt?"

"Just give me your word. I want her to have my share."

"Hell, it's too early to count yourself out, Walt."

"Don't give me no bullshit. You know I'm a dead man. Now give me your word."

Fargo hesitated only a moment, then shrugged. "Okay, Walt, you got my word."

"Now kill me."

Fargo pulled back. "You gone loco?"

"No. My head is clear. It's my body from the waist down that's gone. But that still leaves the Apaches with plenty to play with. So you got to kill me, Fargo."

"That's crazy talk," Fargo told him. " 'Soon as Clint or Slats gets back here to give us a hand, we'll get you out of here. Just keep your ass low."

Walt laughed then, a bitter, miserable croak. "Hell, Fargo. They ain't comin' back for us. They figure we bought it by now. That means bigger shares for them."

Walt dropped his head and began to cough dryly.

Fargo knew at once the man was telling the truth. He glanced back up at the rimrocks. The Apaches were still advancing, using boulders and protruding ledges for cover; they were like shadows inching along the canyon, gray ghosts with pale headbands prowling in the afternoon. Fargo thought, I've taught them some respect for my shooting, maybe. There were only five, maybe six, Apaches left.

Fargo uncorked his canteen and held it to Walt's lips. Walt gulped feebly at the water. Then Fargo took a swallow himself, the cold neck of the canteen pulling painfully on his cracked lips.

"You better get out of here, Fargo," Walt gasped, "while you still can."

Fargo nodded. He was thinking the same thing. But he couldn't leave without Walt—or, at least, without at least making another effort to get him out.

Abruptly, two successive slugs struck the ground so close that dirt and shards of rock kicked up into Fargo's face, momentarily blinding him. Fargo flung up his gun hand to protect his eyes, then scanned the rimrocks and saw figures moving swiftly along the rim toward the canyon mouth. If Fargo didn't move out of there fast, they would soon have him cut off.

Holstering his Colt, Fargo grabbed Walt under the armpits and began to drag his deadweight across the open ground toward his Ovaro. With Walt draped over the pinto's neck, Fargo could mount up and make a run for it. But a sudden, concentrated flurry of rifle fire poured down on them, forcing Fargo to leave Walt and take shelter behind a boulder.

The Apaches were too close now—and Fargo would never make it out of the canyon with Walt. He glanced down at the Ovaro. The pony was standing back in among some rocks, tossing his head and occasionally pawing the ground before going back to the grass he was cropping. He was a courageous, powerful animal, but there was no way he could carry both men any great distance—not with a passel of Apaches on his tail.

Fargo looked back at Walt. He was lying facedown in the dust, his fingers digging into the ground.

"Walt!"

The man raised his head.

"Can you crawl over here?"

Walt began to drag his paralyzed body toward Fargo. His progress was agonizingly slow.

As Fargo waited, a slug sang off the boulder inches over his head. Wincing, Fargo ducked lower. "Come on, Walt," he urged.

Walt glanced up. "I told you, Skye. I'm paralyzed. Leave me."

"Shit! I don't want to do that, Walt."

"You ain't got no choice. You stay any longer, they'll get you, too!"

Fargo squinted up at the rocks. Walt spoke the truth. He glimpsed one Apache not a hundred yards above him. Before the Indian ducked out of sight, Fargo saw the Indian's face clearly, his anthracite eyes shining in his broad pan of a face. Before Fargo could lift his Colt, the face vanished.

"Kill me, Fargo," Walt pleaded. "Don't leave me to these devils."

Fargo felt cold sweat standing out on his forehead. He knew he would be doing Walt a favor, but that didn't make it any easier. Painfully, unhappily, he drew his Colt and aimed at the man staring up at him.

"Don't forget your promise, Fargo."

"I won't! Now turn your head, dammit!"

Obediently, Walt turned his head and closed his eyes.

Aiming carefully at a spot just behind Walt's ears, Fargo pulled the trigger.

It took only one shot.

Afterward, riding up the canyon astride his Ovaro, Fargo comforted himself with the thought of just how much more merciful for Walt that single, annihilating bullet had been when compared to the slow, terrible death the Apaches would have visited upon him.

It was some comfort—but not much.

The Apaches, mounted up as well, were hard on his tail, their Spencers blasting, slugs whining off the rocks around him. The Apaches knew the herd was gone, but cheated of Walt, they now wanted Fargo to hang facedown over a fire.

The canyon trail became rapidly steeper and then turned into a series of tilted slab rock benches that rose to a narrow pass. The afternoon's slanting sunlight left a hand of shadow along the west wall, but the heat was undiminished. It sucked moisture from Fargo's shirt and crusted the soapy lather on the Ovaro's sweat-stained neck. Fargo peered up at the narrow slot of the pass and wondered if the Ovaro would be able to make it that far.

But he lasted, as Fargo knew he would. Dismounting at the first outcropping of rock that offered protection, Fargo tied the mount to a clump of manzanita, lifted his Sharps from the saddle scabbard, and dropped a linen cartridge into the breach. Slamming up the trigger guard, he settled down behind a low boulder to wait.

But the Apaches had halted nearly a quarter of a mile down the canyon. They had seen him dismount and knew well enough how easy it would be for Fargo to hold them off from this high vantage point. There was a long interval of waiting as the frustrated Apaches milled about, palavering. Abruptly, the decision went to Fargo as the Apaches broke and raced back down the canyon and out of sight.

Fargo climbed up onto a rock to watch the dust settle back on the trail behind them. When he was certain they were gone, he mounted back up and headed after the herd, his angry thoughts now centered on the remaining three men of his outfit who had made no effort to ride back to give him and the others a hand. The plan had been for Fargo, Walt, and Rifkin to hang back and slow the Apaches—with the others to return as soon as the herd was safe. Before leaving Fargo and the others, Clint, Slats, and Yank Mosely had promised Fargo they would do just that.

But the trail ahead of Fargo was empty of riders. Not one of those bastards had turned back. Walt had been right. The men were interested only in seeing an increase in their share of what the herd would bring.

Now that he was out of danger, Fargo allowed his exhausted pinto to plod slowly along. Soon it was night, and he didn't realize he was dozing until he almost tipped out of the saddle. Remembering a night-herd trick an old-timer had taught him, he loosened his holster belt to the last hole, then looped it around the saddle horn. It held him snubbed tight to the pommel.

The last thing he remembered before falling off to sleep was his blood oath to Walt Tennyson—an oath he intended to keep.

Exciting Westerns by Jon Sharpe from SIGNET

**Buy them at your local
bookstore or use coupon
on last page for ordering.**

Exciting Westerns by Jon Sharpe

(0451)

- [ ] THE TRAILSMAN #18: CRY THE CHEYENNE (123433—$2.50)*
- [ ] THE TRAILSMAN #19: SPOON RIVER STUD (123875—$2.50)*
- [ ] THE TRAILSMAN #20: THE JUDAS KILLER (124545—$2.50)*
- [ ] THE TRAILSMAN #21: THE WHISKEY GUNS (124898—$2.50)
- [ ] THE TRAILSMAN #22: THE BORDER ARROWS (125207—$2.50)*
- [ ] THE TRAILSMAN #23: THE COMSTOCK KILLERS (125681—$2.50)*
- [ ] THE TRAILSMAN #24: TWISTED NOOSE (126203—$2.50)*
- [ ] THE TRAILSMAN #25: MAVERICK MAIDEN (126858—$2.50)*
- [ ] THE TRAILSMAN #26: WARPAINT RIFLES (127757—$2.50)*
- [ ] THE TRAILSMAN #27: BLOODY HERITAGE (128222—$2.50)*
- [ ] THE TRAILSMAN #28: HOSTAGE TRAIL (128761—$2.50)*
- [ ] THE TRAILSMAN #29: HIGH MOUNTAIN GUNS (129172—$2.50)*
- [ ] THE TRAILSMAN #30: WHITE SAVAGE (129725—$2.50)*
- [ ] THE TRAILSMAN #31: SIX-GUN SOMBREROS (130596—$2.50)*
- [ ] THE TRAILSMAN #32: APACHE GOLD (131169—$2.50)*
- [ ] THE TRAILSMAN #33: RED RIVER REVENGE (131649—$2.50)*
- [ ] THE TRAILSMAN #34: SHARPS JUSTICE (131991—$2.50)*
- [ ] THE TRAILSMAN #35: KIOWA KILL (132513—$2.50)*
- [ ] THE TRAILSMAN #36: THE BADGE (132807—$2.25)*

*Prices slightly higher in Canada

**Buy them at your local
bookstore or use coupon
on next page for ordering.**

Exciting Westerns by Jon Sharpe